One Curious Woman

PAMELA H. BENDER

Print ISBN: 978-1-64649-004-2
Ebook ISBN: 978-1-64649-005-9

Year of the Book
135 Glen Avenue
Glen Rock, Pennsylvania

Dedication

To Heidi Glunt
who inspired the story

and

Laura Hershberger and Betzi Baker
whose relationship between sisters
was my model.

Acknowledgments

It's been a few years between books. Then Heidi Glunt, my massage therapist and friend, sparked my creative impulse. Her life, demeanor, adventures, and accomplishments led to *One Curious Woman*. Since Tanner Stoltz is her life-partner, I appreciate his help in my research. Both of them allowed my imagination to run free as I developed the plot.

I love to write, not edit. That's where the following people came to my rescue: Sandy Gordon, Barbara Shepp, Beverly Stiffler, Demi Stevens, and my daughter and editor, Laura Hershberger.

While writing a book, I live in two different worlds. The following people listened while I shared fictional events of the day: my husband Joe Bender and Alice Errickson.

Thank you, Demi Stevens, my publisher, for turning my typed pages into a book.

A book is just letters clumped on pages without you, my readers. You bring my characters to life when you visit their imaginary world. I appreciate the time you spend with them. Thank you.

A short conversation with a stranger
can change the direction of your life.

One

"Rose? Is that you, Rose?" the old man whispered without opening his eyes. He reached across his bed, and Willow automatically slipped his cold hand into hers. She gently closed her fingers. The man's lips opened to let out a sigh of relief.

Willow stroked the pale skin. *He's dehydrated. No wonder they can't get a blood sample*, she reasoned. She repositioned his hand and elbow so she could look at his upper arm. *He's been stuck too many times*. She stroked his upper arm with her free hand, thinking, *His veins are collapsed*.

His eyes opened and saw a stranger. She was a young woman, pretty, without a trace of makeup. Her light brown hair looked as though it had arranged itself as it fell just above her shoulders. Her olive-tone face looked peaceful, relaxed, and stress-free. Mr. Stark noticed that her full lips didn't curve into a fake smile. He liked that. Two big dark-brown eyes connected with his and didn't look away. Willow raised one brown eyebrow very slightly as if to ask a question, but she patiently waited for him to adjust his thinking to the situation. Mr. Stark appreciated her sensitivity and admitted, "I was with Rose. I thought she'd come to get me."

Willow nodded her head, understanding his disappointment. After a few minutes, she patted his hand, and he noticed hers was small with neatly trimmed nude nails. "The hospital sent me to get a blood sample. My name is Willow. It's nice to meet you, Mr. Stark." He sighed a useless protest, while she sat quietly. She smiled, picked up a glass from his bedside table, and positioned its straw to his lips. "I need you to drink some water. It will help me find your veins," she encouraged.

He took two small sips, struggling to swallow. "Is that enough?"

"That's enough," Willow said, replacing the glass on the table and reaching into her bag. "I'm going to slip this elastic band around your arm."

"It won't do any good," he warned. "I'm too old."

"I've been told, I have a magic touch," Willow stated, as she prepared her needle. "This will only take a minute, so hold still."

His eyes widened as the vial on the needle filled with blood. "Look at that!" he exclaimed. He studied Willow as she completed her tasks. "You're good at your job. Your parents must be proud of you."

"I don't think they give it a thought," Willow admitted. "It's just my job."

"I'm glad they sent you. Can you sit by me?"

"Of course," Willow answered, as she settled back in the chair.

"I like your name, Willow. It's different," Mr. Stark said. "Are you named after the willow trees?"

"When my dad told my grandma that I was a girl, he asked her to come to the hospital. Grandma said that she would as soon as she planted a baby willow tree."

"Your grandma was a wise woman," Mr. Stark said with a chuckle. "My wife was named Rose after the sweet-smelling flower.

You remind me of Rose," he admitted. "She had a quiet stillness like you. Most people talk too much."

Willow nodded in agreement.

"I visit with Rose and others." He shrugged his shoulders and sighed. "I'm ready to join them."

Willow nodded, then responded, "The people here will miss you. You have quite a fan club."

"I don't mean to complain. They're good to me, but I'm stuck in a rut. Every day is the same. I need to be free." He tilted his head, adding, "Ruts are boring."

"I get the feeling you and Rose led an exciting life."

He closed his eyes and whispered, "Yes. Life with Rose was never boring. We had adventures."

Willow packed her equipment, snapped her medical bag shut, and looked back at the patient. His loving expression confirmed that he was revisiting Rose. She walked out, heading to the next name on her list.

"I'm done," Willow said, handing the head nurse her copy of the list. "I got samples from all six of your patients."

"I don't know how you do that," the nurse admitted. "You have the knack, that's for sure." She looked down at the list and crossed off one name, initialing the change. "You don't have to test Mr. Stark's sample. He passed away half an hour ago. He was a nice man."

Willow nodded, sighed and walked out. A balmy breeze met her at the front door and accompanied her on the walk to her car. Once her bag was in the trunk, she turned to face the breeze. It refreshed her, clearing her senses from the institutional smells of the senior-living residence. Her head tilted back to catch the sun's warm rays on her face. Her body reacted with goosebumps. It'd been a cold spring in South Central Pennsylvania, filled with grey days and chill winds. It was the second week in May, but the weather was just warming up. She closed her eyes, inhaled deeply, held it for four counts, opened her mouth and exhaled as if she was in her yoga class. It centered her.

Willow checked her watch and felt a wave of regret thinking, *I still have to stop at the hospital to drop off the blood samples. The sun will set before I get back home. This beautiful day will be over.* She climbed behind the wheel, turned the key, and heard her old car, Bumper, chug to life. *Why do I keep driving back to my parent's home? I waste three hours a day, gas money and Bumper can't take much more.* A shiver ran up her spine as she realized, *I'm in a rut.*

Tracy was changing into her street clothes as Willow walked into the hospital locker room. They were the same height, five feet two inches on a good day, but both of them were athletic, strong, and fit. That's where the similarities ended.

Tracy had long, natural blonde hair that she kept in a loosely wrapped bun when working in the hospital. When she wasn't, she wore it in a ponytail held by her favorite denim scrunchie. Her skin was pale ivory, and all her features were more delicate, her lips a pale pink. Her eyes were as big as Willow's, but they were crystal blue.

She looked at Willow and asked, "Want me to throw your uniform in the wash with mine? I have two machines now."

"Yes, thanks," Willow said, as she opened her locker and grabbed her jeans and tee shirt. "I had an epiphany today. I've been living my life in a rut."

"What caused this big revelation?" Tracy asked, sitting down on the bench while Willow took off her uniform. "Have you finally been thinking about what I told you?"

"A sweet old man said he was ready to die because he was stuck in a rut, and ruts are boring," Willow explained before pulling her clothes on. "I think I'm in a rut. I've decided to get a place of my own. Did you say the farmer is getting ready to rent another trailer on his land?"

"Yes, he is," Tracy said, as she began rummaging through her purse looking for her phone. "Jim, the farmer, buys two old trailers every fall. He puts them in one of his barns and he and his wife, Carla, work on them during the winter. They take them apart, fix and paint everything, install working toilets that hook up to his lines and rent them out in the spring. Ours was the first one he brought out, and we love it. This trailer will be the last one for a year."

"Will they rent to a single woman?" Willow asked.

"It's small. Jim and Carla will have to rent it to a single person. I saw it last night and took a picture to show you. If I could just find my dumb phone," Tracy said in total frustration.

"Check the front pocket. Sometimes you shove it in there," Willow suggested.

Tracy followed Willow's suggestion and found her phone. While she turned it on and located the pictures, she said, "As soon as I heard it was going to be set up in the grove of trees, I thought of you. You love trees." She shoved the phone toward Willow. "Look! It's painted green with blue trim around the windows. It's a 1969 Aristocrat Lo-Liner with all new wall coverings, cushions, and upholstery. Carla even made curtains for the windows. It has a new stove and refrigerator. I memorized all the facts because they're setting it up today for an open house tomorrow. It'll be gone before noon."

Willow stared at the picture and saw the potential. "How much is the rent?"

"I asked Jim, and he said because of the size, it would cost less than ours. You can afford it, and the rent includes utilities," Tracy promised. "I told Jim and Carla that my best friend might take it, and he said you can see it tonight. I couldn't sleep all night I was so excited, but when I told you, you didn't seem interested," Tracy complained. "It's because of Roland, isn't it? You two never got along in high school."

"I hardly know the man," Willow said, "but he made it clear that he didn't like me. It doesn't matter, because now you're dating him. You and I are like sisters, so if you like him, I do too. If you love him, I'll learn to love him. But if he makes you cry or breaks your heart, I'll give him a good reason to hate me."

"And you're learning how to be at peace with everyone?" Tracy teased. "How's that going?"

"Look's like we're about to find out," Willow said shrugging.

"I thought Roland was the reason why you didn't want to see our trailer," Tracy admitted.

"Not really," Willow clarified. "I didn't want to barge in on your private life. We've been inseparable since we were kids, but now that you and Roland moved in together it's different. Who wants a third wheel hanging around?"

"Are you kidding? I'd love it if you moved in. It's not like it's just Roland and me living on the farm. There are eight other trailers in our park, and Jim and Carla plan to expand each year. Roland is always hanging out with his new buddies. Come see! Tonight's Friday, so we'll be gathered around the firepit. We'll grill up some hamburgers and hot dogs, sing songs and dance."

Willow picked up the phone and studied the picture again, saying, "If it has trees around it, it sounds like heaven. I won't have to hike every weekend to get out in nature."

"That's not all," Tracy promised, her blue eyes wide in excitement. "You have a thing for rocks; farmers hate rocks. There are piles of them all around the farm. You can have all the rocks you want."

"I'd respect your privacy. How far is this trailer from yours?" Willow asked.

"It's a half mile down the path. Besides once spring comes, you'll be off hiking. I'm just lucky we work together, or I'd never see you," Tracy complained. "I may have Roland, but the forests have you."

"Is there a place to hike in that area?" Willow asked, grabbing Tracy's shoulders.

Tracy nodded and stood up. The two women placed their hands on each other's shoulders, just as they had when they were little kids. "Just walk out your front door, head toward the woods and you'll meet up with the Appalachian Trail," Tracy explained, and they both hugged in celebration.

Willow dialed home while heading out of the hospital. "Hi, Mom. I won't be coming home tonight. I didn't want you to worry."

"Thanks for calling," her mom answered, and then waited quietly in case her daughter wanted to share more information. The thoughtful pause reminded Willow of her conversation with Mr. Stark earlier that day. She'd never noticed that her mother's pattern of speech was so similar to her own. Willow wondered if their courteous behavior was the reason they never fought. Once Willow had reached maturity, her mom rarely asked questions. Their relationship had slowly shifted into good friends who dearly loved and supported each other. That's why Willow had felt comfortable living at home for the past three years.

"I've decided to move here, so I don't have that long commute," Willow explained.

"Good! I don't like you driving this far, especially in the winter," her mom, Laurel, replied.

"There's a trailer on a farm that's just been overhauled. I can rent it cheaper than an apartment, and it's in the woods. Tracy and her boyfriend moved into one a few months ago. She says that mine will make ten trailers on the farm. Because I'm Tracy's friend, the farmer said I can come to see it tonight. If it's not rented tonight, they'll have an open house tomorrow, and it'll be gone in hours. They're having a bonfire tonight, so I'm going to spend the night. I have my sleeping bag."

"Sounds like fun. You and Tracy have always been two peas in a pod."

"Roland's her pod now," Willow reminded. "My trailer would be a half mile up the trail from hers. I'll send some pictures if I get it."

"You deserve it. You've been saving for your own place for three years," Laurel reminded her.

"Let's hope it all works out," Willow worried.

Tracy hadn't exaggerated. The farm was less than ten minutes from the hospital. From the top of the hill, she could see the trailers nestled in the valley. She searched for one in a grove of trees and spotted it, surrounded by a few people. Willow stepped on the gas and drove quickly to the farm.

When she arrived, a woman and two men were sitting at a picnic table outside the door of the trailer. She heard the man say, "I love it, but it's up to her. She'd have to get rid of a lot of her stuff."

Willow asked the woman, "Are you Carla? I'm Tracy's friend, and I'm very interested in renting this trailer. May I go in?"

Carla stood and shook her hand. "Nice to meet you. I thought this couple was Tracy's friends."

"No, I work with Roland. He told me about it," the man explained. "I never met Tracy."

Carla smiled at Willow, saying, "I'm glad you came. Tracy said you were as close as sisters." They both turned, startled by the sound of slamming doors from inside the trailer.

The woman stuck her head out and yelled to Carla, "Where is the closet? I can't find a closet. There's no room for clothes."

Carla told Willow, "Let me go in first. I'll see if his wife is done." Once inside, Carla opened a small door and showed the woman, "It's here."

"What! You've got to be kidding," she shrieked as she headed toward the trailer door. "Can you move?" she asked Willow. "I need to leave."

Willow stepped aside. "There's no real closet. Don't waste your time!" she warned as she rushed past.

Willow stood in the doorway and looked around the space. It was cozy, warm, and inviting. It was everything she'd hoped for. "I love it," Willow announced.

Carla asked. "Do you need more closet space than this?"

Willow laughed, "Not me. I'm a minimalist. Well, almost. I have twelve articles of clothing, not the eight they recommend." She ran her hands over the peach walls and looked into the small bathroom. "Is this a shower?"

Jim joined them, answering, "Yes. This trailer is farther than the others from the community building, so we put in this fiberglass bathroom unit. The shower, sink, commode, and floor came as one piece. According to that other woman, the closet space is an issue. How much do you need?"

"She's a minimalist with twelve pieces of clothing," Carla bragged. "Does that include your shoes?"

"Yes, I have sneakers and my hiking boots," Willow explained. "I think there's still a pair of black flats in the trunk of my car, but I don't count them. I spend most of my free time hiking," Willow explained.

"A woman connected to the land, like Jim and me," Carla announced, smiling.

"More to the forests," Willow clarified. "I love trees and rocks."

Jim looked up and joked, "We're all about dirt and crops. Trees get in the way, and rocks drive me crazy." Jim was pushing the center bed cushion back toward the wall. She watched as a hinge bent, and half the cushion became a back for the couch. He sat on it and reached down to lift a table top secured to the wall. A leg unfastened, and suddenly there was a table surrounded by cushioned seats. He motioned Willow and Carla to join him in the newly formed booth. "Do you have a boyfriend like Tracy?" he asked.

"No! I'm twenty-one and don't want one for at least ten years," Willow explained. "There's too much I want to do."

"Won't you be afraid out here in the woods all by yourself?" Carla asked.

"No, weather permitting, I'm off hiking by myself every weekend. My sleeping bag and backpack are all I need."

"You're a pretty woman. Aren't you afraid someone will take advantage of you?" Jim asked.

"We have two daughters. He's very protective," Carla explained.

"I carry bear spray, mace, and a hunting knife strapped to my leg," Willow assured. "I have my checkbook with me. I don't want to lose this place. I love the location."

"Don't you have questions?" Jim asked. "Propane is used for the heat, stove, oven, and water heater. They'll top it off once a month. Everything else is electric. Did you see how I moved the bed to become a couch?"

"Yes, I can do that. Tracy told me what you want for rent. It's fair. She said it includes all utilities and the trailer is hooked up to your water, sewage and electric lines."

"That's right," Jim answered. "We rent it by the month. People move in and out of trailer camps. You have to give me one month notice if you want to move. I have the same responsibility if I want you to vacate the trailer."

"That's fair," Willow agreed. "I saw two trees outside. Would I be allowed to hang my hammock? I'd have to install hooks in the trees."

"That's all right with me. I was going to cut the trees down. The picnic table comes with the trailer. Some people get a grill to cook outside," Jim explained. "You have to be more careful. You're in the woods, and it's spring. The bear cubs might smell food cooking and pay you a visit. Their mother will be right behind them."

"I have my cook stove in Bumper," Willow explained. "I've cooked on that for years when I camped, but never when there were cubs around. I'm looking forward to having a real stove, oven, and my own refrigerator."

"Is your car named Bumper?" Carla asked, still curious.

Willow nodded. "My grandma was Lenape Indian. Native Americans believed in *animism*, that spirits live in inanimate objects. She named anything she valued. I name things too, have since I was a little girl."

"I thought Indians had straight hair. Your hair has some curls?" Carla asked.

Jim gasped. "Now why would you ask her that?"

Willow laughed and answered, "I got my curly hair from my dad's side of the family. Mother Nature is my hairdresser. If it rains, my hair gets really curly. If it's dry and windy, it only curls a little."

Carla grabbed Jim's arm and urged, "Let's rent it to Willow. Last night Tracy told me her best friend would love this trailer. I'm glad it was you and not that other woman. You remind me of Tracy."

Jim answered, "Seems you've won the approval of my wife. Any other questions?"

"Can I hang up a clothesline?"

"Sure, but we provide two washers and a dryer in the main building. We also have a bathtub and two shower stalls for women, one for men. My wife insisted on the bathtub for the little kids that live here, but anyone can use it. You're welcome to use all the facilities."

"We need to put the name of the trailer on the lease. We haven't thought of one yet. Any suggestions?" Carla asked.

"I'd name her *Fern* because she lives among the ferns and wildflowers."

When the lease was signed, and the check handed over, Willow asked, "May I spend the night? Tracy said there's a group getting together around the firepit."

"There's no sheets or blankets on the bed. No soap or towels either," Carla said, looking around. "The trailer doesn't come with any pots, pans or tableware."

"I have my sleeping bag and backpack in Bumper. I have everything I need. This is a luxury I'll have to get used to," Willow admitted. "Tomorrow I'll bring all my clothes and my late Grandma's household items."

Two

Willow lowered the tabletop, reached under the couch and pulled out a lever. The cushion released and dropped down to convert into her double bed. She spread out her sleeping bag, took off her boots, and laid down. *This is a better mattress than the one at home,* she realized.

With her hands under her head, Willow looked up and noticed that the ceiling had been painted periwinkle blue. A breeze blew through the open windows, making the curtains flutter. *This is heaven,* she decided.

Willow sat up and went through her bag, selecting what she needed for the night. A journal, flashlight, toothbrush, toothpaste, soap, towel, bear spray, mace, and knife lay on top of her bed.

The remaining items in her pack included underwear, jeans, a long sleeve shirt, and sweatpants. She thought of the times she'd slipped crossing a cold stream, had her arms bitten up by bugs, or slept in sweatpants by a campfire. *Even if I have my own home, my backpack is my lifeline when I'm hiking. I won't unpack these clothes.*

Tracy had sent a congratulatory text and the time for the cookout. Willow thought, *News must travel fast here.* She checked her watch and was relieved to have an hour to herself. She unrolled her yoga mat, watching as it cleared the walls and lay flat. Willow sat on it cross-legged, one hand on each knee with the thumb touching the index finger. She closed her eyes and focused on her breathing. She felt centered. In a few minutes, her attention turned to the new sounds of her home. The electric heater hummed and the trailer creaked as if it too were settling into new surroundings.

Willow formed the yoga Butterfly Pose by placing the soles of her feet together, leaning over, letting her head hang down while her hands reached out beside her feet. The tension in her spine released. She spent forty-five minutes enjoying the sensations from other yoga poses done in sequence.

The trailer key slid into the slot and locked it. Willow had strung the key onto a hemp cord necklace and slipped it over her head. *I'll get a couple keys made,* she decided. *One for my parents, one to hide outside, and one for Tracy.*

It was still light, so she tucked both her flashlight and mace into her hoodie pocket and walked down the bluestone road toward the muffled noises.

The trees were filled with the sound of busy birds, moving quickly among the branches, searching for the last feeding of the day. She stopped to identify a flock of migrating blue jays. She remembered that her grandma taught her, *If a blue jay appears in your life, feel safe and protected.* Willow smiled.

A rustling sound in the high grass beside the road caused Willow to turn in time to see a small, spotted deer fawn. A doe immediately trotted out from a clump of brush, walked onto the road and situated herself between Willow and her baby. It pushed the fawn with her nose, and they both disappeared into the thick brush and grasses. *I'm going to love living here,* Willow decided.

The road led Willow out of the wooded area into mowed grass fields, where nine larger trailers surrounded a community building. Willow spotted Tracy standing in a group around the firepit. Her long, blonde hair was blowing around, whipping across her face. *Why in the world is she wearing her hair down? It must be driving her nuts. Maybe she lost her scrunchie*, Willow thought.

Willow remembered that Roland was tall with blond hair like Tracy's. She looked and decided he was the man throwing horseshoes with another group in the meadow. They were loud, some just watching while drinking beer. Each throw caused a wave of comments and laughs. *Looks like a friendly group.* She stepped out of the woods and started down the road toward the gathering. A figure waved. *There's Carla*, Willow thought, as she waved back.

Carla alerted Tracy who left the group to walk toward Willow. They met halfway down the road.

"Isn't this perfect?" Tracy asked, running up to hug Willow.

"It is all you said and more," Willow admitted. "How can you stand your hair flying around?"

Tracy shrugged, saying, "Roland loves it this way."

Willow gave Tracy the side-eye, and they both laughed. "I'm starving. Do I smell hot dogs? Is there enough for me?"

"There's enough to feed an army," Tracy promised. "Let's race."

Tracy took off through the field, her hair floating behind her. Willow was caught off guard, but this was a race they'd run throughout their lives. She burst forward, getting into her stride and slowly closing the gap. The two women were running for the love of running. The crowd, however, was watching and cheering for Tracy. They were both the same height and ran side by side for several minutes.

Willow looked at Tracy and suggested, "Let's end in third gear!" she sprinted ahead, surprised when Tracy didn't keep up. Willow slowed down and turned to find her friend. Tracy caught her off guard, passing her at full speed. Willow laughed as she watched Tracy run into the congratulatory crowd.

"She beat you fair and square," Roland announced, his arm hung over Tracy's shoulder. Willow walked toward the group, still laughing.

"No one can beat Willow," Tracy announced. "She won states two years in a row. I'm the only one, but it's never fair. Willow worries more about me than winning. She always stops to see if I'm okay."

Willow watched Roland's fingers squeeze Tracy's shoulder to stop her compliments. Her friend looked at Roland, shocked by his action. Roland dropped his hand and pulled Tracy toward the grills declaring, "Time to eat. Enough running around."

The conversations flowed naturally. The group was interested in meeting her and providing information about life on the farm. Willow enjoyed the camaraderie. Roland stayed close to Tracy, occasionally leaving her to go in their trailer, returning with another beer. When the men returned to their game of horseshoes, Tracy sat by Willow, asking, "Are you having fun?"

"I am, but I overate. Your friends are generous. How long does this go on?" Willow asked.

"It's Friday, so it'll last till ten or eleven. Did you find your sit-tree?"

"Not yet. I plan to do that first thing tomorrow before I go home and get my things."

"Want to see mine?" Tracy asked.

"Yes, but Roland might be mad if we leave together."

"Oh, who cares," Tracy said, getting up and walking toward the main building. "We'll look like we're using the commodes in the community building." Her answer confirmed Willow's suspicion—Roland was jealous of their friendship.

The community building had several rooms, each kept clean and neat. One place held the washing machines and dryer. The woman's locker room had two showers and two bathroom stalls. A large meeting room was open for residents use. "We have get-togethers here when it's really cold or rainy. Sometimes Carla and Jim rent it out for wedding parties or clubs. It brings in money for repairs."

Tracy walked out the back door and led Willow to a weeping willow tree. She pushed through the bare branches and sat with her back against the tree's bark. Willow joined her. "Did you choose this tree because of my name?"

"You are the one I go to whenever I need to think things through. When I saw this tree, I knew it was perfect. And look at all these branches! When the leaves come out, it will hide me from the world," Tracy said enthusiastically.

"I'm grateful that you thought of me, but it's hard to climb through the branches," Willow pointed out.

"At least it's not an oak. Remember when your grandma told us about picking out our sit-tree?" Tracy asked.

"Don't pick an oak, because squirrels nest in oak trees," Willow recalled.

"And the squirrels will throw nuts at your head if you dare sit under their tree?" Tracy added. "I miss your grandma."

"So do I," Willow admitted. "I'm going to go through her boxes and bring a few of her things to the trailer."

"Bring the dishes with the little trees around them. I love those dishes," Tracy suggested.

"I will. Do you want one or two settings? She loved you like a granddaughter."

"Roland made a big deal out of picking dishes at the Salvation Army store. He's more excited about setting up housekeeping than I am," Tracy admitted.

"He doesn't like me moving here. I can tell," Willow suggested.

"He's really possessive about me. Wants to know where I am all the time," Tracy admitted. "This weeping willow tree is the best hiding place on the farm."

"Grandma would approve of your tree. I'm not sure she'd approve of Roland."

"He's getting better. Living with someone takes a while to get right. I made it seem scary, but it isn't. He just loves me so much," Tracy said, getting up. "I'll show you Jim and Carla's farmhouse." They headed around the corner of the community building. "Look, you can see it in that valley. Isn't it heavenly?" Tracy asked.

It was dusk, but Willow could make out the farmhouse and two big barns. "How much land do they have?"

"Jim is the fourth generation to farm this land. I think he has over a hundred acres," Tracy explained. "He inherited it from his parents when they retired to Florida. I can't imagine being that blessed."

"So here you are," Roland yelled. "Is this the way it's going to be? You two sneaking off from me?"

"Why would we need to sneak off from you?" Willow asked, noting the way he swayed when he talked.

"Because Tracy lives with me now," Roland announced. "We're together here. This is our home. You work with each other all week. Isn't that enough togetherness for you two?"

"I don't plan to invade your private time, Roland. I live a half mile from your trailer. You won't see much of me, but I am a member of this community and plan to attend the events and use the facilities. Can you handle that?" Willow asked.

"I don't have a choice, but don't come to our home. I don't want you hanging around Tracy," Roland insisted. "You two get creepy, always talking about yoga, trees, and rocks. It's stupid shit."

Tracy was furious, "I can invite anyone to our home."

"Anyone but her," Roland yelled.

Willow smiled at Tracy and said, "It's okay. I have my own home. You two need your privacy. It's been a long week, and I've got things to move in. Say my goodbyes to the others." Willow walked on the stone road back to the quiet of the forest.

It was dark when Willow entered the woods, but the moon was full and enabled her to see the road. She loved full moons. Willow remembered all the nights she and Tracy would dance around under the full moon while her grandma laughed and clapped.

Willow sighed, saddened by the happy memory. *They have to work things out,* she reasoned. *It's none of my business.* Willow saw the lights in the windows of her trailer and stopped to admire how cozy it looked nestled among the trees. "I'm home," she said softly.

Willow opened the trunk of her car and took out a small pot, tin cup, box of tea bags and three granola bars. While climbing up the blue steps, an owl hooted, making her hesitate and consider falling asleep under the open sky, but the soft bed and warm trailer beckoned. Willow walked in, closed the door, and enjoyed the luxury of a home with lights, a stove, and a bathroom.

Willow kept a Gratitude Journal. Every night, she listed three things that had made her thankful. The night before, she had struggled to come up with three. The entry read: *I'm grateful for Mom's cookies, hand lotion, and hats.* She smiled as she quickly chose what to write for this day. *I'm grateful that: Mr. Stark taught me "ruts" are boring, Jim and Carla created Fern, and I'm living close to Tracy, in case she needs me.*

Willow put the journal and empty cup on the counter, turned the lights off and slipped into the sleeping bag. Her hand opened the curtains so the moonlight could shine down on her.

Three

Willow had spent the night in a deep sleep. When she rolled onto her back, she sensed her surroundings were different. Her eyes fluttered open to bright sunlight. *What time is it?* She lifted her arm to look at her watch. *8:30? How could I have slept until 8:30?* She turned to her side and studied her new surroundings. The peach walls gave the trailer a warm, peaceful ambiance. Aside from the birds singing in the trees, it was quiet. *It's like sleeping in a cocoon,* she realized.

Willow struggled to get her bearing. *It's Saturday, and I don't have to follow anyone's schedule. If I were home, breakfast would have been cooked and served. I'd have done the dishes, made my bed, and taken a shower. What had I planned to do this weekend?* One day had changed the pattern of her life. She'd been looking forward to something, but she couldn't remember what. *Something Grandma always did.* She sat up, remembering. *It's the herb festival. I was going to plant herbs in the garden.*

Last night, she'd talked with Carla while sitting around the fire. She'd asked her if she could plant a garden. Carla had warned her that the lack of sunlight would make it challenging to raise vegetables in the woods, and anything that did grow would be eaten by the animals. "You live on a farm," Carla consoled her. "What doesn't sell at our vegetable stand, we give to our renters. During the summer, you'll have more vegetables than you can eat."

Willow got out of bed, went to the bathroom and was pleasantly surprised when warm water came out of the faucet. *What luxury,* she thought as she splashed water on her face and began cleaning up for the day. *I need to buy groceries. I'm hungry,* she realized. She put two health bars and a bottle of water in her backpack, slipped it over her shoulders, and opened the door. The morning light illuminated a breathtaking view. *I have to find my sit-tree,* she remembered. Willow walked into the woods.

The night before, she'd asked Carla if there was a stream close to her trailer. She was thrilled to hear there was. Her grandma's sit-tree had been beside a stream, and it was there that she carefully instructed and shaped Willow and Tracy's character. In spring, she'd teach them the names of the plants as they sprung to life. In summer, her grandma would help Willow and Tracy dam up the stream, so it was waist-high when the little girls sat down.

"Always return the stream to the way it was before we came," Grandma demanded as they tore down what they had built. In the fall, they collected rocks, her grandma identifying them by name and properties. "This is jasper, it's easy to carve. We'll make it into a pendant. We need this big quartz rock in the dining room. Quartz is a powerful, soothing stone that can heal both your body and your brain," she'd instructed. In winter, Grandma would fill a big thermos with hot cocoa, and they'd spread a blanket by the tree. She'd watch them tiptoe onto frozen sections of the stream and pretend to skate, then they'd drink the cocoa while throwing stale bread to the birds and rabbits.

Willow followed Carla's directions, hearing the stream before she saw it. She stopped to prepare herself, thinking, *Even if it's just a trickle of water, it will be enough.* She moved through the trees until she stopped in awe. There they were—both the stream and her sit-tree. They were side by side, a thick, mature maple, and a broad babbling brook. She stood staring, enjoying the thrill of something being better than expected. She moved to the tree, slipping the backpack off her shoulders onto the ground. Her grandma had taught them to brail the forest, so she ran her fingers on the bark as she walked around the tree. It was a healthy tree, with thick bark. She looked up to see if it was waking for spring. The longer days of light exposure had begun the process, aided by the warmer weather. Buds were already noticeable.

She sat on a soft mound of soil, leaned against the bark and let out a deep contented sigh. She focused on her breath to erase thoughts. Her grandma had taught her that a sit-tree was vital because it rooted you in the present. She closed her eyes and focused on the feeling of the tree supporting her back, the soft soil cold against her legs. She sat crossed legged, her hands posed on her knees. She was one with her environment, just being. It was peaceful. When Willow opened her eyes, she felt stronger and refreshed.

Willow reached for her water bottle and health bars. While she ate, she studied the scene before her. Small sprigs were sprouting up around her. The moss was still brown, and she looked forward to watching it turn bright green. She looked for signs of poison ivy or sumac vines, but this tree had none. She moved her focus to the stream and how some spots in sunlight glistened. She stood up to get closer. The water looked about ankle deep, still running fast from the torrential downpours further north. She knelt beside it, reaching through the cold water to the rocky bottom. Her fingers touched a few small rocks, and she lifted them out of the water. *I'll make these pendants,* she decided, letting thoughts move from the present to the future. A squirrel ran along the bank, stopping still when seeing her. It sat up on its haunches, its tail jerking in alarm. They watched each other until the squirrel scampered away.

Willow sat back down by the tree, took her cell phone out of her coat pocket, and checked to see if she had service. She Face-Timed her mom, Laurel, whose features appeared on the screen, saying, "Good morning. I loved the pictures you sent us. Fern looks like a perfect home for you."

"I'm really enjoying it. Is dad there too?" Willow asked.

"No, he's got big plans to take over your garden," she said laughing. "Who knew he wanted it? He's rototilling as we speak. It's amazing what he does now that he's retired."

"I'm glad he's having fun," Willow said. "I wanted to show both of you, but I'll show him pictures when I get there. Look, Mom! I found my sit-tree. It's by a stream."

Willow moved the phone, so her mom could see the water. She held it still for a few minutes, so Laurel could both hear the rushing stream and see the sunlight flickering on the surface. Then she moved it to show her own face leaning against the tree. Willow asked, "What does this remind you of?"

"Grandma's sit-tree," Laurel answered. They talked for a few minutes, Willow explaining her plan for the day. "I'll have lunch ready for you. See you soon," Laurel promised.

Willow and Laurel walked into one of the out-buildings, Orange Cat right behind them. When they opened two collapsible chairs and sat down, Orange Cat jumped on Willow's lap, purring loudly. The women looked at the seven boxes lined up against the wall. "I feel funny going through Grandma's things," Willow confessed while petting Orange Cat.

"We're lucky she wasn't a packrat," her mom answered. "Grandma never kept anything she didn't need."

"The less you have, the less you have to take care of," Willow quoted.

"She'd be happy to know you could use some of it," Laurel encouraged, as she pushed her straight brown hair behind her ears.

Willow studied her mom, noticing how much they looked alike. Laurel was a few inches taller than Willow, still thin and athletic at sixty-three. Willow got her olive skin and athletic ability from her mom. Willow put Orange Cat on the floor and opened the box marked *Kitchen*.

"Put what you want along the wall. Don't feel you have to take it all today," Laurel suggested. "We never use this garage unless your father has plans for another retirement hobby."

"Everything I touch has a memory," Willow said. "I can fit three settings of her dishware. Tracy was hoping the boxes had this set with the little trees," Willow said as she placed them in the *to-go* box.

"Would Tracy like some?" Laurel asked.

"I offered, but it seems Roland is into setting up housekeeping together. They picked out a set from the Salvation Army," Willow said shrugging.

"I can understand that," her mom answered. "His family life was difficult. He must be so happy to have someone as sweet as Tracy."

"I hope she's happy with him," Willow confided. "Do you see the box with the hammock?"

"It's the biggest box. Let's push it against the to-go wall," Laurel suggested.

Willow returned to the box marked *Rocks*. "I'll find room for all of these. What I can't fit in the trailer, I'll put around the garden as Grandma did."

Orange Cat jumped on the box and rubbed against Willow's face. They both laughed. "She's used to having you around. She missed you," Laurel commented. "I'm worried you'll miss being with Tracy. Is it hard for you to share Tracy with Roland?"

"He made rules. Roland decided that we have enough time together at work. When she's home, that's his time with Tracy."

"Is that going to be difficult for the two of you?"

"Not for me," Willow said. "Now that I moved, I'll have three more hours in the day. I'm looking forward to doing more hiking. I'm only a few miles from the Appalachian Trail. During the week, I plan to spend a few nights finishing my yoga instructor certification. I emailed my teacher, so she's got me set up with an instructor in Carlisle. I only need twenty more hours."

"Good! What's next on your list?" her mom teased. "You're always looking for new experiences."

"I'm still thinking about getting certified as a massage therapist. I can set up my own hours, have my own clients, and do a job that helps people. Sticking needles into people's arms is not my dream job," Willow admitted.

"You'd be wonderful at that," Laurel encouraged. "You have a healing touch. Remember when you and Tracy volunteered at the nursing home? The head nurse said both of you were a *Godsend*."

"I'm not in a rush," Willow admitted. "This summer, I plan to spend my weekends at music festivals and craft shows. I'm going to sell my hemp necklaces, rock pendants, decorated horseshoes, and natural oils."

"That sounds like fun. I thought Tracy was going to do that with you?"

"I doubt Roland would allow it. He's never liked me," Willow said. "He's always gone out of his way to be mean to me. I don't know why."

"Don't you?" her mom said softly.

Willow looked at her mom in shock. "What are you talking about?"

"Don't you remember? The parents were invited to watch the eighth graders end-of-year races. You'd all taken the tour through the high school to get ready for the next year. You came onto the field, looking so excited and proud. It was the first time you were running on the high school track. It was in June. Don't you remember?"

"I do. It was fun. We had a great time," Willow said. "But I don't remember Roland being there."

"Remember the last race of the night? It was supposed to be funny. They picked the tallest boy to run against the shortest girl," her mom reminded.

"I think I ran that race," Willow said, still uncertain.

"You did," her mom confirmed. "Roland was the tallest boy. The crowd laughed when the two of you started down the track, his long legs against your little ones. It was the first time we'd seen his dad come to an event. He was a surly, cruel man."

"I won the race, didn't I," Willow said, suddenly remembering. "Was that Roland?"

"Yes, and the crowd was on their feet, amazed at how fast your little legs were moving. You took three strides to one of Roland's. Your dad and I saw Roland's father smack him across the face and call him a loser," her mom explained.

"That's sad," Willow admitted.

Four

It was four o'clock when Willow turned her jam-packed car onto the farm lane. She drove slowly, avoiding dips in the gravel road. Tracy must have been watching for her because she waved her down at the community building. "What's up?" Willow asked.

"Roland didn't mean what he said last night. He was a little drunk. He feels terrible about it," Tracy explained.

"Don't worry. I'm happy living here. I want you to be happy too," Willow explained.

"What in the world is all this stuff?" Tracy asked, sticking her head in the open window.

"I bought groceries; it was fun. The rest is my stuff from home and Grandma's boxes," Willow explained.

"I wish I could come to help you unpack. I'd love to see Grandma's things. She was the best."

"I'll have you come over some other time. We better not push the issue with Roland. I don't want him to resent my living here," Willow admitted. "I better go. I bought frozen pot pies, and I don't want them to defrost."

A few yards up the road, she passed Roland. He ignored her. His eyes were squinted, his jaw clenched as he focused on Tracy, waving goodbye with a look of longing. *She knows I'm home if she needs me,* Willow reasoned.

The food was the first to be unloaded. It was comforting to see the empty shelves filled with provisions. When the CD player and discs were unpacked, her favorite music eased her concern for Tracy. Willow's clothes came next. Her dad had been a Navy man, so he'd shown her how to roll clothes to save room and avoid wrinkles. She placed the rolls in one row on the bottom of the closet, stepped back, and realized it was wasting precious space. The clothes could fit into one of the kitchen drawers. The cabinet was located close to the trailer door, so Willow decided to use it for her coat and backpack. She rolled her jacket, then put the bag on top, with the pocket holding the mace open for quick access.

Willow went outside and unpacked her camping gear. Jim had shown her an empty compartment that'd been designed to hold spare tires. She slid in her camping and hiking gear. Her dad had insisted she take a shovel, rake, and a metal box filled with his idea of essential tools. Willow slid them in next to the camping gear, making sure there was ample room for her grandma's hammock, Jasmine. *Just barely,* Willow worried. She took Jasmine out of the box, rolled her as tightly as her clothes, and pushed her in. *I'll set you up when I have more time,"* she promised, before shutting the door.

She felt in her pocket for the copies of her keys from the hardware store. Willow tried all three of the trailer key copies. They all worked. *I'll give one to Tracy to bury under her sit-tree.* She sat in Bumper, turned the new car key, and heard the engine come to life. *Thank goodness you're an old car whose keys can be made at a hardware store.*

Willow decided she was getting hungry, so she carried the box marked *kitchen* into the trailer and laid it on the table. She'd washed everything in the to-go boxes in her parent's dishwasher, while her mom put her grandma's linens in their washing machine. With everything clean, unpacking was easy. The plates, bowls, glasses, and utensils were placed in kitchen drawers or cupboards.

The cookware was in another box and once unpacked, she put some to work. She plugged in the ancient toaster and plopped in two pieces of bread. While that cooked, she filled her grandma's teakettle with water and turned on a gas burner. She'd enjoyed her trip to the grocery store. In the spice aisle, she'd spotted a red McCormick sugar and cinnamon bottle. It made her crave one of her favorite childhood snacks, cinnamon toast. She opened the new spice container and tub of margarine. The toast popped up, and the memory of her grandma's voice flickered, *Use the wooden tongs, so you don't get electrocuted.* She opened her drawer and took out the old tongs, noting the burn marks on their tips. She placed the slices on one of her plates.

The warm toast had melted the margarine, sugar, and cinnamon by the time the teakettle whistled. The high pitch brought back fond memories. *I haven't heard that since Grandma died.* Willow turned it off, reached into the cupboard, and took down a cup and saucer. When she sat down and saw the little green trees on the dishes, it triggered an emotional ache in her heart. *How long has it been,* she wondered, as tears welled up. *Three or four years?* She picked up the toast and took a bite. It was just as delicious as it had been in her grandma's kitchen, and that eased the ache. She ate it all.

On the floor next to her chair was the box marked, *linens.* Her mom had wrapped something in the two matching kerchiefs Tracy and Willow wore whenever they went into the woods. *Cover your head, so the ticks don't get in your hair,* her grandma would warn. Willow lifted the article out, and carefully unwrapped the scarfs. She smiled when she recognized the little tin sign that read: The Sun's Out! Let's Go on a Hike! Willow remembered her grandma asking,

"Is the sun out?" Willow and Tracy would run out the door, tilt their faces to feel the sun, and if it felt warm, they'd yell, "Let's go on a hike!"

Willow felt a twinge of excitement, similar to the thrill she'd felt when they'd head off to the woods. She used her cell phone to check tomorrow's weather. *Sunny with a temperature in the mid-sixties.* Willow slipped her hand into her jean pocket and took out a business card with a phone number. She called it.

"Trail Shuttler," a deep voice announced.

"Hello. I was given your business card at a hardware store. I need to hire a shuttler to drive my car from the Regional Office of the Mid-Atlantic Appalachian Conservatory to the Carlisle AT parking lot by the Route 11 overpass," she explained.

"Sure, what day are you going?" he asked.

"Tomorrow morning. Is that possible?"

"No problem. It's a short, seven-mile hike on flat terrain. Is this your first hike on the AT?" he asked.

"Yes, it'll be my warm-up hike. I'm going to purchase my Appalachian Trail Passport and read up on the Leave No Trace rules. I understand the office opens at 10:00 on Sundays."

"It does. I have a shuttler taking a car from the Carlisle AT parking lot at around 9:00 right to the AT Regional Office. Give me your cell phone number. He'll call you when he gets there. Make sure you have a credit card, extra car key, and enough gas for the trip," he explained.

"I will. Thanks for your help. I'll call in advance from now on," Willow promised.

"You'll need to. The longer hikes require more advanced notice," the driver explained. "What's your name and license plate number?"

When Willow hung up the phone, she sat and stared out the window thinking, *I'm going to hike on the Appalachian Trail.* Willow remembered all the stories her grandmother told about her 2,200-mile hike with her grandpa. They weren't married yet, because her grandma wasn't sure it was a good idea to marry a man who wasn't at least part Indian. She was unwilling to give up her connection to nature and her tribe's customs. Her grandpa had suggested the trip. It was shocking, back then, for women to hike the trail, but her grandma had jumped at the chance. They used heavy, surplus military equipment, and clothing. She recalled the trip as the best six months of her life. *I let myself fall in love on that trail,* she always said. When Willow was in high school, she'd asked what she'd meant by *letting herself fall in love.*

Her grandma had sat down, looked across the table and looked into Willow's eyes, before saying, "This is important, so listen closely. Too many women let themselves fall in love with the first man who shows up. Now that makes no sense. Don't even think about falling in love until you know it's a good fit. Make sure the man values and enjoys the same things you do. Don't get taken in by one of the fakers. There was no way your grandpa could have faked his love for nature on the AT. That man really enjoyed a good climb up a steep pile of rocks."

Willow wondered why Tracy hadn't been there. Then she remembered, Willow's parents had taken Tracy to visit her mother in the hospital.

Willow arrived at the regional office before it opened. The box outside the office supplied hikers with trail information. She sat down on a bench, reading pamphlets and listening to the hikers sharing stories and tips. When Willow's phone rang, she stood up, walked to the parking lot, and introduced herself to the man leaning against her car.

"This old car's been around for a while," he said.

"But it keeps on going, and it's filled with gas. Here's the key, and my credit card."

He opened the door, sat down, and started the car. He took out his phone, typed in her numbers, and stuck it out the car window for her signature. "It'll be on the left side of the Carlisle AT parking lot. You'll cross two overpasses, and you want the parking lot after the second one. I'll leave the key under the rug in the backseat because everyone looks under the driver's rug. Any questions?"

"Is tipping allowed or expected?" she asked.

"Thanks, but my price includes a tip. Have a good hike," he called out, as he backed up and headed out of the parking lot.

Willow turned and noticed the doors to the office were open. A shiver of excitement ran up her spine. Fifteen minutes later, Willow fastened the orange AT Through Hiker Pass to her daypack, wrapped her hiking-scarf around her hair, and walked a quarter mile on the side of Route 174. When Willow saw the wooden sign that read *APPALACHIAN TRAIL—Maine to Georgia*, she stepped into the woods following the path north.

Willow's daypack held three bottles of water, sunscreen, a peanut butter sandwich, two health bars, guide book, and a few band-aids. She carried her bear spray and phone in the pockets of her cargo pants and her knife strapped to her ankle. It felt freeing to take the first AT hike without the heavy backpack and trekking poles she used on overnight hikes. The path was free of rocks, soft, with patches of dried mud now and then. There were no clouds, just a light breeze, a sharp contrast to the reports of bad weather for hikers in Georgia. The hikers in the Regional Office expressed concern for friends who were hiking where it was raining hard and fast. The rock climbs would be slippery, the flat trails water-logged and muddy. She wished she had asked her grandma more about her trip. How much had it rained? What weather did she experience? Willow had watched hikers use one of their trekking poles to extend their cell phone while recording videos of their experience. *I'd rather keep a written journal of each day I hike the trail,* she decided. With that in mind, she found herself noticing more details of her own experience.

The trail was clearly marked with about ten-inch-long white stripes on trees, posts or fences. Willow relaxed and got into her fast-paced strides. She'd always enjoyed navigating uneven ground on hikes and trail running. It worked different muscles in her hips, knees, and ankles. She knew these were the muscles that would reduce the risk for over-use injuries to her joints from walking all day on the man-made hospital floors.

The hike was mostly flat but never dull because hikers had to cross public roads. It took restraint to stop, look, and listen for traffic. When the trail left the woods, it cut through lush farmland. She tried to imagine how many hikers walked this path to keep it so clear of weeds or crops. The farms were so large that only the sounds of nature could be heard. She wondered if the farmers gave the AT their permission or the trail had the right-of-way. Regardless, she felt tremendous gratitude for the opportunity to experience the beauty of their land.

She sat on a log beside an open field to drink water and eat the sandwich. Several turkey vultures circled over her head, giving her a good view of their red and black heads. Several times, the trail crossed animal grazing land. Four wooden steps up and back down enabled the hikers to cross over the wire fences. Willow was accompanied by slow grazing cows in one beautiful meadow. They seemed mildly curious, their big brown eyes watching her walk by while they chewed their food over and over again. In one cornfield, she looked up to see a range of mountains in the distance. *Someday soon, I'll hike up there,* Willow decided.

The path returned to the woods, and Willow heard the sound of traffic moving. *The overpasses are close. I can't believe the hike is almost over.* Willow stopped, took out another bottle of water and a health bar. While she ate, she shook her legs to see if her muscles were feeling the strain. *Yup, I'm going to be stiff tomorrow. I'll go to a yoga class after work. I have to meet my new instructor, and I'll need the workout. Maybe Tracy will join me. It can't hurt to ask,* she decided.

The first overpass shocked her back into the fast-paced world of civilization. The cars sped under her as she walked on the steel bridge with thick wire sides. The second overpass was longer, and in the middle, the American Flag had been tacked to the wire siding. When cars beeped, out of respect to their flag, Willow filled with pride for her country and gratitude for the National Park. It had been a beautiful day for a hike.

Five

"You've already changed; you must have come in early. Did you have a nice Sunday?" Willow asked as she changed into her uniform in the locker room.

"I couldn't sleep last night, so I got up early. Yesterday wasn't a great day," Tracy admitted. "I baked a chicken, but Roland said it was too dry. The baked potato was half raw. The meal was a mess."

"Tell him to put gravy on the chicken. When I was at the grocery store, I saw all kinds of gravy in jars," Willow suggested, "or tell him to cook the next meal."

"It doesn't work that way," Tracy explained.

"What doesn't work that way?"

"Men and women," Tracy said shrugging. "They expect the woman to cook, do the laundry, clean, and all that house stuff."

"Mom works just like you, so Dad helps with household chores. What does Roland do?" Willow asked.

"He takes care of the cars, tracks how many miles we get to the gallon, keeps them gassed up and all of that. He pays the bills and carries the groceries for me."

"How does he pay the bills? Does he use his money?" Willow asked.

"No, we combine our money now that we're living together. Roland uses it to pay for everything," Tracy said casually.

"How do you pay for the things you want? You probably make more than he does."

"If I need something, I just ask him for money. He's usually pretty decent about it. He told me he makes more than I do because he does physical labor," Tracy said.

"That doesn't make any sense, but it's really none of my business. I shouldn't pry. It's just that I wanted to invite you to join me in a yoga class tonight. I'm going to meet my new instructor, and I really need to stretch my muscles. I hiked on the Appalachian Trail yesterday."

"You did?" Tracy asked. "I can't wait to hear about it. How many miles?"

"Just seven. I hiked from Boiling Springs to Carlisle. I'll tell you after work," Willow promised. "I think you can take a free class at the studio. They usually let new members try it out. Come with me tonight."

"I'd love to. I haven't done yoga since I moved in with Roland. I'll text him and see if he says it's okay," Tracy said.

"Why does he have to give you permission?"

"That's how it works with most couples," Tracy said shrugging. "You work as a team."

Mondays are always hectic for lab technicians. So many blood samples have to be taken that they're prioritized by urgency. It took Willow's mind off her concern for Tracy until she went into the women's public bathroom near the waiting room. She was in the stall, looked up, and read the poster on the back of the stall door. It was a long list of "red flags" to help people identify a potentially abusive person including *controlling all the money*. She took out her phone and snapped a picture of the list.

Willow felt physically ill. Her hands shook as she washed them. *Tracy wore a long sleeve uniform today, and she changed early. Maybe she's hiding bruises. He's isolated Tracy. He's already limited Tracy's time with me. If I say too much, too soon, he'll come between us. Maybe I should tell Tracy to read the poster.* She checked, and each stall had the same notice.

The bottom line of the poster said, "Create a Safety Plan and get connected to a local organization."

Willow was comforted, knowing she could be Tracy's emergency plan. She remembered the trailer key she'd made for Tracy was in her backpack, so she headed toward the locker room.

"It was crazy today," Tracy said, already changed into her jeans and another long sleeve shirt.

"It sure was," Willow agreed. "I even had to take blood from a woman in the waiting room. I don't do that often."

"I did one the other day. It's usually to see if the patient is pregnant," Tracy said. "I'm not going tonight. Let me read you Roland's text. *'If you're going to stupid yoga, I'm going to a bar with the guys. I might as well eat there too. You decide'*."

"I texted him back that yoga isn't stupid. My shoulders and back ache all the time since I stopped going," Tracy read. She looked up with a sentimental smile. "Look what he texted back."

She handed over her phone, and Willow read, "Sugarplum, if I had known that, I'd have given you massages every night. Come home, and I'll show you how much better I am than yoga."

"Sugarplum is his pet name for me," Tracy announced with a glow.

The only mild reaction Willow could come up with was, "Why Sugarplum?"

"Roland says that he loves the fact that I'm so mellow and agreeable. He thinks it's sweet. His parents were mean. I've seen the scars from his father," Tracy confided.

Willow opened her locker and took out the extra key to her trailer. She'd put it into a plastic tube from the hospital. "Please don't tell Roland about this key. It's our secret," she urged. "Bury it under your sit-tree."

"I can't keep secrets from Roland. What would I say if he found it before I buried it?" Tracy asked.

"Put it in your purse," Willow suggested.

"He goes in my purse. He checks to make sure I have a few dollars or my car keys, stuff like that," Tracy admitted.

"I'll take this key," Willow said, pausing to control her anger. "I'll bury it under your sit-tree. It'll be under one of Grandma's white quartz rocks. It's just there as an emergency plan. Whenever you want, go to my trailer. In the closet by the door, I keep mace."

Tracy looked away from Willow and back down at the last text from Roland. "I don't know why you think I need the key and mace. It's a little dramatic, isn't it? Roland loves me with all his heart." She looked up, suddenly angry. "You can keep your stupid key. I don't need it."

"I'm still going to put it there," Willow insisted. "What if I'm sick or I need you to come to help me?"

"Oh, I hadn't thought about that," Tracy answered, her expression softening. "What's the mace for?"

"I live in the woods. Mace protects you and me from just about anything," Willow suggested.

"I'd like to have one of Grandma's rocks under my sit-tree. She loved quartz rocks, said they were the most powerful of all minerals," Tracy admitted. "It's up to you if you bury it. I don't want to hear any more about it. I won't keep secrets from Roland. We tell each other everything."

Unconsciously, Tracy pulled down one of her sleeves as if she was cold. The action convinced Willow she was hiding a bruise. She'd done the same thing when she lived with her father and mother.

Willow sat, waiting for her to start their usual chatty conversation. She didn't, and the strained silence was deafening. Tracy stood up and gave a half-hearted wave goodbye before walking out the door.

Willow watched her leave, stunned by the realization that Tracy had chosen Roland over her. A wave of sadness hit her. She sat looking at the door, hoping Tracy would come back. It took her several minutes to realize Tracy was gone.

Willow had called earlier in the day to make an appointment with her new yoga teacher. It surprised her how comforting it was having somewhere else to go, rather than her trailer. She dressed in her black yoga pants and a tee shirt, relying on her coat to cover her as she left the hospital. She'd gone online and looked up the studio, her teacher's certification and experience. The picture of a smiling woman sitting in the cross-legged meditation pose seemed to fit her name, April Braden. An impressive bio listed fifteen years of experience, her certification, and both the school and teacher she had learned under. The class schedule and varied offerings indicated she ran a well-developed yoga studio.

The studio was a fifteen-minute drive from the hospital, in a building that looked like it had been a small hardware store. The sign read, "Mindful Living Yoga Studio." She parked and walked up to the purple front door. When Willow walked inside, the gentle aroma of lavender, the soothing spa music, and the decor created a peaceful environment. The sharp contrast to her stressful life shocked her. *I needed this*, Willow realized.

April was waiting and welcomed her by placing her hands together, her fingers pointing upward against her chest. She bowed and softly said, "Namaste."

Willow was taken aback and muttered, "Thank you."

April smiled, saying, "You must be Willow Hunt. I've been looking forward to meeting you. I'm April."

"Nice to meet you," Willow answered. "This atmosphere is calming."

"I'm glad you sensed that. We want all our yogas to feel refreshed and leave with a feeling of bliss," April responded. She pointed to a book saying, "Everyone signs in when they arrive." Willow signed in before April took her for a tour of the facility explaining, "We have lockers for your belongings and shower facilities to get ready after class. You can rent or borrow a mat and towel each time you practice if that's more convenient."

April led her to one of the yoga classrooms, explaining, "I have a forty-five-minute class starting soon. You're welcome to join us. The members of this class come directly from work and need the more restorative style of Yin or Hatha Yoga. Does that interest you?"

"Yes, definitely," Willow said. "My yoga classes have been limited to one studio, in a converted garage that could only accommodate ten students. This is a very different experience for me."

"Well, I'm glad you came. Your teacher speaks highly of you. I understand you want to complete your yoga teaching certificate. I have an hour break after this class, so we could talk then. Do you have time?"

"Yes, I'll look forward to it," Willow answered.

"Good, you can put your things in a locker. I'll see you back here in around fifteen minutes," April suggested.

April began the class the same way she had greeted Willow. She stood quietly, waiting for everyone to settle down. She smiled, placed her hands together, and said, "Namaste."

Everyone in the class took her same pose and returned the greeting saying, "Namaste." Willow joined in, feeling a positive energy and spiritual connection among the group.

After class, April introduced Willow to the other students and guided her to a small room. "Please sit down," she said, motioning her toward a velvet, purple couch. "I'm going to have a cup of my Yogi Tea. May I pour some for you?"

"It smells delicious," Willow admitted. "I'd love some."

"If you like it, I'll give you the recipe," she said, handing it to Willow. "I'm going to change the topic of our conversation. I look forward to talking about working with you to complete your certification another time, but I need to address your stress level. You're well trained in Yen poses, but I noticed you favor your right side. You also seem to have pain in your legs. Am I right?" April sat down next to her on the couch.

"Thank you for noticing. My muscles do hurt. I hiked seven miles on the Appalachian Trail on Sunday, and Mondays are busy at the hospital. So many patients need blood samples taken after the weekend," Willow explained.

"Did you hike alone?" April asked.

"Yes, I usually do. It was an easy hike," Willow said. A quiet pause encouraged her to continue speaking so she added, "I called an

AT shuttler Saturday night and Sunday they picked up my car at Boiling Springs and left it for me at the Carlisle AT parking lot." After another pause, she added, "My grandma and grandpa walked the entire Appalachian Trail before they were married."

"How interesting. I was surprised you called today," April admitted. "Your teacher said you called her on Friday to say you were thinking of moving to Carlisle. Did you find a place?"

"I did, and I moved in Saturday," Willow said. "I rented a renovated trailer on a farm, just a few minutes from the hospital. The farmer and his wife add two each year."

April sat quietly, prompting her to continue. So Willow added, "There are ten on the farm now. Mine is by itself in the woods, so it's peaceful there. I found a sit-tree. It's right by a beautiful stream, and I have two trees where I plan to hang my grandma's hammock."

"So you like it?" April asked.

"I do," Willow said.

"Did you move in all your things?" April asked.

"I'm a minimalist, so I don't have many things. Most of what I brought from home belonged to my grandma. She passed away a few years ago."

April put her tea down and looked at Willow. "If I train you to become a yoga teacher, I will teach you about empathetic listening. You'll learn to listen at a different level, with the ability to understand the feelings of the other person. This is what I heard from you. You thought about moving on Friday when you called your yoga teacher. That may mean you value your yoga classes. You rented a place and moved all your things from your home on Saturday, which may mean you found the perfect place. Most of the things you moved belonged to your grandma. That night, you arranged to take a seven-mile hike by yourself on the Appalachian Trail the next day. Is that right?" April asked.

Willow stared at her and blinked as tears ran down her cheeks, "Yes," she whispered. "I sound like a chicken running around with its head off."

"Not at all," April said, smiling. "You sound like a woman who is moving out on her own, who hasn't grieved for her grandma. Were you very close?"

"Inseparable. My mom and dad worked long hours. I spent most of my time with Grandma," Willow said, wiping her tears away. "She was a Lenape Indian and the leader of our family. Grandma was wise, gentle, and grounded by the forest she lived in."

"You were fortunate. Your grandma must have been a spiritual woman," April decided. "I look forward to working with you, but not just yet. You need to put your roots down in your new home. Continue doing yoga, but move it outside. Spend time by your sit-tree, breathe, and meditate there. Hang up your grandma's hammock and enjoy all the memories."

"I haven't even finished unpacking her things," Willow admitted. "Now I know why."

"Yoga isn't just physical postures or asanas. I believe its purpose is to unite the mind, body, and spirit. If you want me to train you, you need to focus on yourself for a few days. Take your time. Call me when you are ready."

Willow nodded and said, "Thank you. I will. You've taught me so much already." She held her hands together and said, "Namaste."

Six

With the recipe for Yogi Tea in hand, Willow stopped at the grocery store. When she turned toward spices, she saw Roland. He was walking up the aisle with a confused expression on his face. She approached him, saying, "Hi Roland. How are you?"

He looked up, took a step back, then explained, "Tracy texted me to stop and pick up two things. I haven't found them yet."

"This is only my second trip here, but I'd be glad to help if I can," Willow offered.

"Don't bother. I can handle it," Roland said, turning away.

Willow thought, *Maybe this is an opportunity.* She called out to him. "I'd like to help because I need some help from you and Tracy."

Roland turned toward her, his face showing interest. "What help do you need?"

"I want to hang up my grandma's hammock, but it's a three-man job. I don't know how high to put in the hooks until we hold it up. I have hooks, but they need to be twisted into the tree. Can you help?"

"I could," Roland stated, shrugging.

"It shouldn't take too long."

"We have plans, but everything Tracy cooks has no flavor so I need a jar of chicken gravy and a box of Stove Top stuffing," Roland complained. They started walking toward another aisle. "I thought you were going to yoga tonight. Tracy wanted to go along."

"I've already gone. The class only lasts forty-five minutes."

"I thought they went on for hours," Roland admitted. "I guess Tracy could have gone."

"She seemed more interested in getting home to you," Willow suggested, hoping to break the ice.

He winked before boasting, "She's always got plans for me… if you know what I mean."

Willow held her composure, ignoring the sexual innuendo. "I think the gravy is on aisle four," she suggested. When they turned down the aisle, she let him find it.

"I got it," he said. "Now I need Stove Top Stuffing. Where's that?"

"I'm not sure. Maybe it's in the next aisle," Willow prompted.

He rushed ahead of her. As she approached, he announced, "I found it." With one item in each hand, he walked straight at her, forcing Willow to move out of his way. "I told you I didn't need your help," he bragged as he walked by.

Willow watched him stride up the aisle toward the registers, carrying brown gravy and pork stuffing. He never looked back. *He's dumb, and he's a bully,* she recognized. *Tracy hasn't seen it yet. She always championed those in need.*

Willow returned to the spice aisle to get her Yogi Tea ingredients. She pulled out the recipe and read: 5 cinnamon sticks; 4 fresh ginger root slices, 20 black peppercorns, 15 whole cloves, 20 cardamom seed pods (press with the back of a knife to release the seeds from the pod. Only use the seeds), 1 black tea bag, 2 quarts of water. Boil for at least half an hour. Pour through a strainer or cheesecloth as you put it into a container.

That seems simple, Willow decided, *but I need a container and a metal strainer.*

The sun was setting as Willow returned to her trailer. Remembering April's advice, she didn't go inside, but sat down at the picnic table and watched the blue sky between the trees turn yellow, orange, gold and purple. She spotted squirrels and rabbits foraging around the trees. The birds had settled into their nests. Just a few doves could be heard cooing.

Her mind began listing all the things she should do tonight: *unpack boxes, put a pot pie in the oven, make Yogi Tea, pack lunch.* Willow stopped herself, and began focusing on the beautiful show nature was putting on. She concentrated on her breathing until she felt one with her surroundings. She too was settling down for the night.

Tracy greeted Willow the next morning with her usual zest, saying, "I heard you ran into Roland last night. He said he offered to help you hang up Grandma's hammock. See, I told you he was a good guy. I'm glad you two are getting to know each other."

"I asked him, but he didn't seem interested."

"Roland says he has to screw the hooks into the trees. See, it's nice to have a man around," Tracy added as she changed into her uniform. "How did yoga go? Roland said you only stayed for an hour. He said I could go every once in awhile if I want."

Willow looked at Tracy's arm and noticed four faint black and blue marks probably made by Roland's fingers. She chose not to pry. "The studio is amazing, like nothing we've ever seen. April is the owner and head teacher who pointed out things I hadn't realized. She noticed my body was straining from the move on Saturday and the hike Sunday. April said I need to take a few days to adjust to my new life and grieve for Grandma. She suggested that I hiked to avoid unpacking her things. She's right. I still can't believe Grandma's gone."

"Neither can I," Tracy said, sinking down on the bench near Willow. "We never talked about it. It's just too painful, especially how she died."

Willow was shocked. "The way she died is the only thing that makes me feel better."

"What do you mean? She died in the woods. They said she was there for days," Tracy reminded.

"What do you mean died in the woods? She wasn't alone. She was camping with Mom. Grandma knew her death was coming, and she wanted to spend her last days in her forest. Grandma went to sleep under the stars holding Mom's hand. It was perfect. She didn't want to die in a hospital."

"I can't picture Grandma in a hospital away from her woods," Tracy recognized.

"I should have moved in with her," Willow said. "I should have seen how weak she'd become."

Tracy shook her head slowly. "We only see what we want to when it comes to the people we love. I'm a perfect example of that."

"I'm here if you ever want to talk about it," Willow suggested.

"I'm figuring it out," Tracy admitted. She stood up and turned back to Willow, saying, "I just remembered the story Grandma told us of how her mom walked into the woods to meet nature. Remember? Maybe she meant she walked away to die in nature."

Willow sat and stared at Tracy. "Maybe it was one of the old customs of her tribe? She hated Grandpa's funeral. She took his ashes home in a jar. The next day I stopped by and asked where she put it. She said she threw the jar away after she freed Grandpa to be with nature."

Tracy got tears in her eyes. "I've been terrible to you. I should have helped you unpack her things. I'm sorry. I would've loved that, but Roland wouldn't allow it."

"Don't feel bad. We're both adjusting to our new lives, that's all. Last night, while my chicken pot pie baked, I unpacked almost all Grandma's things. I just have the box of rocks. April said to *enjoy the memories*. So every time I took something out of the box, I'd think about her and how she used it. It turned out to be a sentimental but lovely evening."

"Did you find room for everything?" Tracy asked.

"Yes, Fern looks perfect now."

"Fern?" Tracy asked. "Did you name the trailer, Fern?"

"Yes, it's even on the lease."

"I should know what you named your trailer. We're losing connection with each other. I don't know anything about your hike on the AT. There's never enough time, because of Roland's stupid rules. He doesn't get what little time we have together when we're at work. He doesn't understand that we're like sisters," Tracy suggested.

"You'll get to see Fern when you come to hang up the hammock," Willow suggested.

"Good luck with that," Tracy admitted. "Baseball season started and basketball finals are being played. Roland comes home, grabs a beer, and plops down in front of the TV. If it's a long night game, I have trouble sleeping with that stupid TV going all the time."

"I don't know how you do it. We hear TV all day at work. Yesterday one woman tried to tell me I should come back later to take her blood because her *stories* were on." They both broke out in laughter.

"It's going to rain all night. What will you do cooped up in the trailer without TV?" Tracy asked.

"What would Grandma have us do?" Willow teased.

"Wash our cars," Tracy answered. "Remember how every time it was raining, and the weather was warm, Grandma would tell us to go out and wash Bumper?"

Willow laughed and remembered. "She'd say, *Don't waste all this water*. I'm glad you reminded me. I'm going to stop at the Dollar Store and buy a bucket and sponge. I've got a bottle of dishwashing soap. Bumper hasn't had a good washing in months."

"Roland washes our cars," Tracy said, disappointed. "He says that's his job. What'll you do after you wash Bumper?"

"I have my laptop, and Jim gave me the password to get on the farm Wifi. Several women at the yoga class recommended a Netflix documentary about the origins of yoga. I'm going to watch that. Otherwise, I'll read. After work, I'm going to the library, sign up for my card and pick up a few books. I need to get inspired. I want to start painting little rocks so I can sell them at the music festivals."

"I'm envious. That sounds like a great evening, and I want to go the music festivals with you like we did last year."

"We still can," Willow suggested. "Did you tell Roland about our plans for the summer?"

"I did when we started dating," Tracy remembered.

"Just assume that he knows we're still doing it, then you can help me make things to sell, while he watches baseball."

"I will," Tracy decided. "We had so much fun while we made good money. Whatever I earn at the concerts will be my money. Roland won't get any of it. I better go. Have a good day," she said before heading off to work.

After work, Willow changed into just her leggings and a tee shirt. Her jacket covered the fact that she wore no bra.

The rain was coming down in sheets when Willow arrived home, so she took off her jacket, grabbed the supplies from the Dollar Store, and stepped into the rain. She tilted her head and let it beat down on her face and body. It felt refreshing.

Willow remembered how Grandma could never understand why people ran inside during a good rainstorm. She always said it was the perfect time to weed the garden, and wash the windows, outside furniture and her hair. She'd put buckets out to collect the rain to use when she scrubbed her floors. Her grandma was always grateful for whatever Mother Nature sent her way, and Willow followed her example.

When Bumper was soaped up and rubbed down, Willow stepped back and watched the rain rinse the car. She was sopping wet when she headed toward the front door. She opened it, looked around, and stripped naked before she entered the trailer.

The rain falling on the metal roof of the trailer was as soothing as spa music. She climbed in her little shower, the warm water a welcome change. It was early evening, but Willow decided to take advantage of her newfound privacy and get into her nightgown.

She'd planned to have a salad but decided this was a night for tomato soup and a grilled cheese sandwich. *It's my home, and I can do whatever I want,* she gloated. *This is the life!*

Two hours later, she was laying in bed, propped up by pillows, enthralled in the documentary on yoga. When it was over, she turned off her computer, threw the pillows on the floor, and fell into a sound sleep.

The next morning the birds were singing, the rain had stopped, and the sun was shining down. Willow woke up feeling connected to her surroundings. She lay there appreciating how peaceful her life had become. Tracy's situation was not, and that worry made her sit up in bed and start planning. *The rain probably made it easier to bury Tracy's key. I'll put the shovel in the car and find a quartz rock in Grandma's box. Tonight, on my way home, I'll pull in by the tree and bury the key. Roland doesn't get back from work as early as we do so he won't see.*

Tracy was waiting for Willow in the parking lot. "I've made up my mind," she explained. "After we eat, and Roland sits down to watch his sports, I'm coming to your house, and we're going to hang Grandma's hammock. She'd want it that way. Grandma always said, *'Women can do anything when they work together'.*"

"I'd love that, and so would have Grandma," Willow agreed, as they walked arm in arm into the hospital.

During the day, as Willow traveled around the hospital, she noticed how many patients were submitting to unnecessary medical procedures because their families couldn't let go. She thought of Mr. Stark, and how he'd yearned to join his wife and family on the other side. By the end of the day, she felt as though a heavy weight had been lifted off her shoulders. *Grandma crossed over with nature. She's with Grandpa and all her relatives now. I'm glad I didn't interfere with her process and her customs.*

Later, Tracy and Willow spread out Grandma's hammock, checking it for holes. "How old is Jasmine?" Tracy asked.

"Grandpa bought it for her when I was born. So Jasmine is twenty-one, like us. He wanted her to have it so we could take naps together under the trees."

"All three of us would nap together, once Grandma started babysitting me. I can still remember the first day, and I was only four," Tracy recalled. "She said we were family because you and I were meant to be sisters. Both of us were big surprises for our parents."

"We were," Willow admitted. "Only children of older working couples. They loved us, but we didn't fit in their lives. Grandma was our godsend."

"Roland's messed up because he never had someone like her," Tracy suggested, as they marked the tree for the hooks.

"You're probably right, but it's not your job to fix him," Willow hinted.

"Where are the hooks?' Tracy said, changing the subject.

"In the metal box on the picnic table. Dad said to use the hammer to bang the hook's end into the tree as far as we can. Then we're supposed to slip the screwdriver in the hook and twist it into the tree," Willow explained. "I was afraid that it would hurt the trees, but Jim said I could. He said he'd planned to cut them down, so the hammock was actually saving them."

"Grandma would love that," Tracy admitted.

Fifteen minutes later, the colorful hammock swung between the trees, its height perfect. "Isn't Jasmine beautiful?" Willow sighed. "It's like she's come back to life after four years in a cardboard box."

"I've never seen a prettier hammock. Jasmine's in a class by herself," Tracy agreed. "Let's see if we can both still fit."

They got in and stared up at the trees and blue sky. "I'm glad we did this together," Willow said, "and I'm glad you like Fern."

"I can't tell you how happy I am that you live here on the farm," Tracy confessed. "It's been difficult getting used to Roland and his ways."

Tracy had just finished saying that, when they heard Roland's truck pull up. He pulled as close to the hammock as possible, opened the window and looked down at the two women. "Am I interrupting something?" he sneered.

Tracy turned her head calmly and answered, "Just two women celebrating a job well done." She carefully got out of the hammock and asked, "Are the games over?"

"No, I'm missing the best part because I had to come to get you. Get in!" Roland demanded.

Willow remained in the hammock as the truck sped down the road. She worried, *I should have told Tracy that I buried the key. It's there if she needs it.*

Seven

The next day after work was the first chance for them to be alone. They walked together to the parking lot. Tracy was as talkative as usual. "Thank you for Grandma's rock. I saw it last night when I was in my sit-tree. All the branches have buds; I can't wait to see him with all his leaves."

"You've decided that your sit-tree is a male?" Willow asked, astonished. "I thought it reminded you of me."

"It does, but I need someone strong to protect me," Tracy announced.

"It doesn't have to be a man," Willow said, looking at her. "From the time you were a kid, you always idealized Dolly Parton. Her poster hung on the wall of our room."

"You're right," Tracy admitted. "Dolly could hold her own with anyone," Tracy said. "My willow tree with Grandma's rock under it is going to be named Dolly. It's like having all three of the strongest women I know protecting me."

"Four strong women," Willow said. "If you ever decide to stand up for yourself, like you do for everyone else, you'd be the strongest of us all."

"Don't worry about me. I've got things under control," Tracy promised. "Roland yelled the whole way back home from your house. When he parked, he started dragging me into the trailer, but I broke away. I took off, running in the opposite direction. Roland can't catch me, so he didn't try. I didn't run to my sit-tree, I ran for the tree line at the border of the farm. I hid there until I saw Roland give up and go inside. That's when I went to Dolly," Tracy explained.

Willow remained calm, realizing Tracy was confiding to her. "Did your time at the sit-tree help you figure things out?"

"I thought so, but when I got home, Roland was sorry. He had turned off the TV and was sitting in the dark, sad and upset. When I walked in, Roland jumped up and threw his arms around me. He promised not to yell anymore, to start taking me on dates, and turn the TV way down low if it's a late game," Tracy announced, proudly.

Willow sat, looking up at Tracy.

"Isn't that great?" Tracy asked.

"Remember yesterday, when I told you about that woman who wanted me to come back after her *stories?*" Willow asked. "We both just laughed. That's because we were trained not to allow patients to treat us that way. Remember what our instructor said?"

"Yes, *teach people how to treat you,*" Tracy said, slowly.

"Did you ever teach Roland what is acceptable and unacceptable to you?" Willow asked.

Tracy leaned against her car and thought awhile. "I never teach Roland anything. He does all the talking," she admitted.

"Why?" Willow asked.

"He never asks. I can't picture him listening long enough for me to tell him," Tracy added.

Willow didn't say a word.

"I'm afraid he'll get mad," Tracy finally admitted.

"Next time you go to the sit-tree ask, *What would Dolly do?*" Willow suggested.

Tracy looked down at her hands, admitting, "It's not that easy. He accused us of having a *thing* for each other."

Willow's hands shot to her hips. "Doesn't he have a good friend? Does he know we're like sisters? Did you tell him how Grandma took care of both of us from the time you were four years old?"

"No, I never told him. He hates you, something about a race," Tracy admitted. "In the beginning, I was so thrilled that he asked me out I didn't want to mess it up. Later I told him you're my best friend. I thought that was enough."

Willow took a few minutes to reflect on the situation. Finally, she said, "You'll figure this out. I shouldn't interfere."

On her drive home, Willow worried about Tracy. *Why does she put up with him?* At the stop light, the reason became painfully clear. She remembered running to Tracy's house to get her to come out to play. Willow never went inside, not even on the porch. Both Tracy and her mom had forbidden it. Instead, the girls had invented a secret whistle.

Willow smiled when she recalled how they'd developed it. Grandma had come up with the idea. She'd sat there while they made all kinds of strange noises. Finally, Willow made a three-note sound without even moving her lips. "That's the one," Grandma decided. "If you lose each other in a store, you can make that noise, and no one will be the wiser. You girls practice. I'm going to make some lemonade. Call me when you think you've got it down."

The car behind Willow honked, and she realized the light had turned green. She waved her, *I'm sorry,* and drove home. Once there, she walked inside, made a ham and cheese sandwich, packed it up, and put three bottles of water in her backpack. She pulled a large garbage bag out of the box and lifted up Grandma's quilt. Willow went to her sit-tree, the one by the stream, that she'd never revisited or named.

As she walked, she remembered being little, running through Grandma's woods practicing the whistle. They'd hide from one another, and then one would whistle, while the other followed the sound. Hours later, tired and thirsty, they asked Grandma to come out and hear them.

She brought out the lemonade in tall glasses with ice cubes. They drank it down while Grandma talked. "This is not a game," she'd instructed. "You will need this throughout your lives. Never teach this whistle to anyone else. Do you promise?"

They both put their hands over their hearts and promised. They were around six. Willow remembered Tracy was wearing Willow's green and white checked blouse that day.

Willow had walked to the tree in a fog, her mind racing back to another time. Without even running her fingers around the bark of the tree, she spread out the plastic bag and then placed Grandma's quilt on top. The memories flowed as quickly as the racing stream beside the tree.

On school days, Tracy would come to her house in her play clothes and change into one of Willow's dresses. They were the same size. It was just the way it was, *sisters* who lived in different houses. After school, Tracy would come home with Willow and change into her play clothes. They'd play for hours, and if Tracy's mom called, she'd eat dinner with them and sometimes sleep over. Whenever her mom called, Tracy would never give a hint what was said. She'd say, "Thanks, Mom, I love you so much." Then she'd turn to Willow and jump up and down in celebration saying, "I can eat with you," or "I can spend the night." Willow suddenly recalled the bruises on Tracy's arms, and how she would wave her hand and say, "I'm so clumsy," but she wasn't.

Willow laid down on Grandma's quilt. She thought of her own parents. They never said *No.* Her parents always celebrated when Tracy joined the family. Willow remembered asking her mom and grandma questions about Tracy's home life. They'd insist that it wasn't Willow's business, and instructed her not to pry. *The same words I'm saying to Tracy now,* Willow realized sitting up abruptly. *I'm repeating the pattern.*

Willow reached for her backpack and took out a bottle of water. She stood up and walked around the tree, thinking back to the day Grandma told them about having a sit-tree. They were still little girls. Grandma had made it sound like a magical lesson that only they would know about. "You must pick out a sit-tree that's just as secret as your whistle. Look for one that is out of sight from your home, preferably in the woods, or in a park. Don't pick one on someone else's property."

"Why do we need it?" Tracy had asked.

"A sit-tree is magical. Look for one with deep roots and healthy leaves. When you lean against it, see if it feels like your special place. You'll know when it does. Then we'll name it. That will make it yours," Grandma had instructed.

"All mine?" Tracy had said, jumping up and down. Willow pictured her. Tracy was wearing a brown tee shirt that looked very similar to the one her classmate used to wear to school. It said *Ohio* on it. She remembered that because the year before their teacher read it to them during class.

"Yes," Grandma had said. "All yours. You can only share it with Willow and me. I'll see if it's good enough to be your sit-tree. If it is, I'll teach you the sit-tree ceremony, and you'll name it."

Willow recalled the feeling that this was just for Tracy. She never picked out a sit-tree of her own. She'd asked Grandma if she needed one, and the answer had been, "You can share mine."

"What's your tree's name?" Tracy had asked.

"Nuhema, it's a Lenape word," Grandma had said.

"What does it mean?" Willow had asked.

"One day you will find out, but now it's my secret," Grandma had instructed. They never pushed Grandma, because they both enjoyed the magical way she presented things.

It had taken both of them a long time to find Tracy's tree. They drew circles on a map and showed the possibilities to Grandma. She always asked the same question, "Can anyone see you sitting under the tree?"

In the park, four blocks from Tracy's house, they found a young tree, that looked as though it had sprouted up on its own. No one mulched around its base, no one clipped away the tall grasses. It was down a small hill in a gully. They ran down the slope, Tracy sat down, leaned against its bark, and announced, "This is my sit-tree."

Willow was skeptical because Tracy had said the same thing about every tree she had tested.

Grandma looked at the new circle and decided this tree she would check out, so they climbed in her car, Bumper, and drove to the park. Grandma stood on top of the hill and watched as they walked down. Tracy sat by her tree and looked up. Willow remembered that the weeds hid her from sight. "That's it," Grandma announced. "Come back up."

Once Bumper got them back to Grandma's house, they all settled down beside her sit-tree, Nuhema.

"What do we do next?" Tracy had asked. "I want to name it Hero."

"That's a good name. Whenever you come to your tree, run your fingers around the bark to say hello. While you do that, look up and see if anyone is watching," Grandma explained.

"What if they are?" Tracy asked.

"Then run back up the hill and come back later," Grandma instructed.

"So I keep my tree secret?" Tracy had suggested.

"Yes. When you sit down by your tree, know you are safe. Take time to figure things out. If you can't, go to Willow's house and talk with her," Grandma directed.

That's why Tracy wants me to live here. That's why my parents thought it was a good plan for me to move by her."

Willow sat back down under her unnamed tree, opened her backpack, and took out the sandwich. *I can't remember what happened to Tracy's parents. It's all a blur.* She watched the stream ripple, as it went over the large rocks in its way. Everything suddenly made sense. Willow remembered how proud she was that her family respected each other's privacy, but Tracy's precarious childhood had made them that way. If they had challenged or shamed her parents, they'd never get to see Tracy again.

How did Grandma come to know Tracy's parents? Willow wondered. *I never saw either of them at Grandma's house. I don't think Grandma was ever paid for taking care of Tracy.* Willow reached for her phone and called her mom.

"Hi, Willow," her mom answered. "I was hoping you'd call soon. I miss you."

"I miss you too. Can you and Dad come to my trailer for dinner on Friday? You won't have to wake up early the next day."

"Sounds like you're planning a late night for us," her mother prompted.

"I'll buy a bucket of chicken with all the sides," Willow continued. "There's always a party on Friday night on the farm. We'll eat here, at my picnic table and you can see my trailer. Then, if you don't mind, I'd like you both to go to the party. I want you to see Tracy and Roland."

"The bucket of chicken will thrill your dad. I've had him on a diet lately, but I don't want to invade Tracy's privacy," her mom explained.

"It's time we do," Willow explained.

"We'll be there, honey," her mom answered. "What time?"

Willow walked back to the trailer, carrying her grandma's quilt. She sat down at her table and turned on her laptop. Once on the web, she typed in Lenape Language. A site popped up. Willow typed in Nuhema. The translation to English popped up, *Grandma*.

Eight

"You were right, It's peaceful and private here," her dad, Brian, admitted. "If I could get your mom to retire, I'd buy us a trailer like yours, so we could travel around and see America, just your mom, me and Orange Cat."

Willow was surprised by her dad's suggestion and studied his face to see if he was just kidding. His confident, easy going nature never forced his opinions on anyone. He was three years older than her mother, sixty-five, but he'd worked in construction all his life so he'd always been tan and in shape. He still had a full head of hair but now it was gray. His blue eyes were focused on her mom, watching anxiously for her reaction. Her dad was serious about this suggestion.

"You never told me you'd like to travel," Laurel stammered. "When did you get this bright idea?"

"Ever since Willow told us about her trailer. The other day I went to an RV show, just to look around. I got all kinds of free books and advice on trailer parks around this country," he explained.

"I never thought about retiring," she admitted. "I love working."

"I know, but I have that figured out too," he assured his wife. "We can live in the National Park sites free of charge if we work part-time in one of the park offices."

"Really?" her mom answered, obviously rolling over the possibilities in her mind. "What parks would you want to live in?"

"All of them," Brian announced. "We can visit the seashore, Smoky Mountains, Yellowstone, Glacier, Grand Canyon, Mount Zion. The list goes on and on."

"I've always wanted to travel," she admitted, "but I don't like staying in motels. They charge too much. I can't justify spending that kind of money when we have a perfectly good home."

"I'll show you the books when we get home," Brian promised. "It's just a suggestion. If you're interested, this weekend the RV show is at the York Fairgrounds. We could drive over, and you could see for yourself."

"Okay," she said. "That would be interesting. We'd need a bigger trailer than Willow's."

"Fried chicken with all the sides and a chance that your mom will retire," he said. "I'm a happy man."

"The way this family talks to each other is weird," Willow announced, as she reached down and helped Orange Cat up onto her lap. "We never come out and tell each other what's on our minds. We wait until it's absolutely necessary. Why is that?"

"It's a Lenape thing," her dad said. "Grandpa explained it to me before I married your mom."

"What are you talking about?" Laurel asked. "What is this Lenape thing I don't know about?"

"The women are in charge," he said, surprised she didn't know. "If a man marries a woman, they live with her side of the family. They follow her clan's rules."

"And my dad told you this?" Laurel asked.

"Yes," Brian said. "It's why we talk the way we do. Women have all the power, but they never speak in public. They have their husband or another male explain their view. We all knew Grandma was the decision maker, but your dad told us what she thought."

Willow and Laurel looked at each other and slowly nodded.

"When he died, Grandma would have me explain what she had decided. Didn't you notice that?" Brian asked.

"I didn't, it was a seamless shift," Laurel admitted, looking lovingly at her husband. "Does that mean I get to make the decisions in this family?"

"Yes, but you always have," he said.

"If Grandma told you everything, maybe you know how grandma came to take care of Tracy," Willow asked. "I need to know."

He looked at his wife for permission. She nodded. "Grandma was driving Bumper, back home past Tracy's house. Tracy was a little thing, maybe three or four," he started.

"Four, I bet," Willow interrupted.

"Her father was out of control. Tracy's mother had been beaten, and she was bleeding through her dress. Tracy was trying to protect her mom by kicking her father. Her father was swinging at Tracy, but she was ducking down to avoid his punches. Grandma pulled over and went up on the porch. The man came toward Grandma, but you know what she carried with her?"

"Her hunting knife," Willow answered.

"Yes, strapped to her ankle. She took the knife out and warned Tracy's father to step away from the little girl. We only know this from Tracy's mom. She told us about it," he explained.

"Tracy's father shouted, '*Who do you think you are? You have no right to tell me what to do*'," Brian continued. "Then Grandma told him she was Lenape, and they protect people who are in danger. She ordered him to sit down, pointing the knife. He hesitated, but finally he did. Tracy's mom told Grandma that he wanted to sell or give

Tracy away so his wife could work. Her husband couldn't hold down a job, and they had no money."

Tears welled up in Willow's eyes, but she sat very still, urging him, "Go on."

"Grandma listened, then she took leadership of their family clan. She told him how they were going to live from now on," Brian explained.

"So Tracy went to Grandma's every day while her mom worked," Willow guessed.

"Yes," Brian confirmed. "Her mom was a proud, hard working woman. Her life must have been a living hell, married to that man."

"Why didn't she leave him? She could have taken Tracy and kept her safe," Willow asked

"She believed she could love the abuse out of him, but instead, he became more violent. She had no money, friends, or family. Tracy's welfare became her only concern. Grandma promised to provide a safe haven for Tracy where she could thrive and still see her mom," Brain explained.

"Grandma raised you like sisters, so you'd always have each other. I couldn't have any more children. You were a miracle. We were blessed to have you," Laurel said.

"Why did you go to work after I was born?" Willow asked. "If I was a miracle child, how could you leave me?"

Laurel looked over at Brian, and he explained. "Your mom had three miscarriages. It took a lot out of her. Then you came into this world. Back in the day, we didn't know why your mom was so depressed. Now we know it was postpartum depression. Grandma took care of you and told your mom to get a job for a while. The quarry needed someone to test the drill samples, and your mom knew everything there is to know about rocks. They hired her, and she found her calling. She's worked ever since."

"I understand," Willow admitted. "Does Tracy know?"

"She knows most, but not about Grandma," Laurel admitted. "Someday you will have to tell her. She has the right to know."

"I don't know what happened to her parents. How come I don't know that?" Willow asked.

"Her father beat her mother until she was limp on the floor. He ran out into the street, screaming," Brian explained. "The authorities called us, and we went to your high school and got Tracy. We took her to the hospital, but her mother died before we arrived. Tracy never got to say goodbye. Her father went to jail for manslaughter. He died in prison, from a fight of some kind."

"Why didn't you tell me? How could you have kept this from me?" Willow demanded.

"Tracy made us promise not to tell you. She refused to come home with us until we did," Brian explained.

"I remember the night she told me her parents had to leave town," Willow recalled. "She cried herself to sleep."

"Her father went to jail for her mother's murder," Laurel said. "She never asked to go to his trial, and she never talked about it. We always planned to adopt her legally. A week after they died, Roland showed up at our door, and she seemed to lose interest in our family."

"I never liked him," Brian admitted. "Neither did your mom."

"Why did you let her date him?" Willow asked.

"She was eighteen years old. We couldn't tell her what to do. We didn't want to push her away. She'd been through enough," Laurel said. "You two started the four-week class in phlebotomy, and we thought she'd get over Roland."

"You convinced us, Dad, was that Mom's idea?" Willow asked.

"Yes, Tracy wouldn't let us spend any money on her. The hospital offered the class for free, so Tracy agreed to take it with you," he explained. "You always talked about working in the health care field, so we thought it would expose you to all the options. The hospital guaranteed employment once you graduated, so we thought it would be a good idea."

"As soon as Tracy got a job, Roland showed her the trailer. He insisted she decide between him or us," Laurel complained. "And here we are. Tell us how it's going."

Willow told them about the bruises on Tracy's arms, and the poster identifying an abusive relationship. She showed them the picture of the chart in the bathroom pointing out, "The very first one, says pushing you into immediate commitment. Look at the rest. We know he thinks being a man gives him all the power. He's jealous and possessive and tries to isolate her from all of us."

"He has two personalities," her dad said. "He was polite and soft-spoken when we met him. When I told him Tracy's curfew, he argued with me, told me she could do whatever she wanted. That's two more items on the list."

"Does he monitor her whereabouts, activities, and spending?" Laurel asked.

"Absolutely," Willow said. "Her check goes in his account, and he pays all the bills. She walks around with a few dollars in her purse. If she needs something, she has to explain why before he gives her the money to buy it. He checks her mileage, phone, and whereabouts. The only one left on the list is cruelty to animals. I haven't seen that side of him."

"What do we do now?" Brian asked the two women.

"I need to swing in Grandma's hammock," Laurel said. "Join me, Willow."

They laid down side by side and looked up at the branches in the trees. "How bad is it?" Laurel asked.

"She's already run away from him and hidden in her sit-tree," Willow explained.

"Grandma was such a smart woman," she said, as she took Willow's hand in hers. "We come from good stock."

"Yes, we do," Willow said, leaning over to kiss her mom's cheek. "What would Grandma have us do?"

"Is he coming after you?" Laurel asked.

"No, not yet," Willow assured. "He's trying to keep Tracy away from me, making her choose him over me. It's tearing Tracy apart. I tried to develop a friendship with him, but he wants no part of it."

"Is Tracy saying anything about him?" Laurel asked.

"Very little. She's making excuses for Roland."

"I was afraid this would happen. I asked Dr. Flint from church—she's a psychologist," Laurel said. "She told me Tracy might be trying to redo her parents' relationship. You know, make Roland happy. Do you have a plan started? What is it?"

"I checked the bathroom stalls in one public restroom, they all have that poster. I want to take Tracy there and hope she reads one," Willow explained.

"What if she comes out of the stall with her happy face and ignores it?" Laurel asked. "You'll have to wait until she's ready."

"She knows her father killed her mother, what else does she know?" Willow asked.

"Children know everything that goes on in an abusive house," Laurel explained. "She always knew everything."

"Does she know about Grandma standing up to her father?" Willow asked.

"I don't think so," Laurel admitted. "That might be the way. Sometime when it seems right, tell Tracy about Grandma standing up to her bullying father. She idealized Grandma, and that might give her the strength to stand up to Roland."

"He might really hurt her," Willow cautioned.

"You need to show her those posters before it's too late, then bring her home," Laurel said.

"We both should move back home once this comes to a crisis," Willow suggested.

"Of course. You come right home. Did you sign a month to month lease?" Laurel asked.

"Yes," Willow said, "but there's another problem. I keep telling her that I shouldn't get involved and I don't want to pry. You ingrained that in me from the time I was a little girl."

"No more," Laurel ordered. "Grandma expected you to take care of Tracy. You must be brave and smart, like Grandma, to save her. I think we should go to this party so I can see them in action."

"Good idea," Willow said, and they both carefully got out of the hammock.

Nine

"Let's take Bumper, so we can come back and review what happens," Willow suggested. "We don't plan to stay."

"Great idea," her mom responded. "It's like taking Grandma along. Come here, Orange Cat. You'll want to see Tracy too."

Most people had eaten, so the men were out in the field gathered around the horseshoe pit. The women were cleaning up, talking, or helping the kids grill marshmallows. "It looks like a nice place to live. Have you made any friends?" Laurel asked.

"Not really. Carla and Jim own the farm. I like them, but I wouldn't call them friends. I've been careful to give Tracy and Roland space," Willow explained.

"Now that I see the children, I want you to spend more time down here. If Roland thinks he's going to lose Tracy, he might encourage her to get pregnant. Look at her over there with the children," Laurel directed.

"I never thought of that, but Roland might," Willow exclaimed. "I'll do laundry tomorrow, and I could start taking showers down here," Willow stated.

"Brian, I'd like a shower in our RV," Laurel said. "It wouldn't have to be big. A shower like Willow's would work."

"You can pick out any RV you want," Brian promised.

Willow walked beside her parents, with Orange Cat cradled in her arms. The children spotted the cat and let out a loud squeal. Tracy looked up and yelled, "I can't believe my eyes." She ran to them, flinging her arms around Laurel.

Willow bent down and let the children pet Orange Cat while fielding questions. "Is this cat yours?" a boy asked.

"This is Orange Cat. She lives with my parents. When Tracy and I were growing up, she was our cat too," Willow explained.

"Don't let go of the cat, 'cause she might run away," one boy warned.

"That's up to her. We let her go wherever she wants. She usually stays close to us," Willow explained, as she put her cat down. Orange Cat walked around the children, rubbing against their legs. When she spotted Tracy, the cat trotted toward her.

"If she comes back, can we pick her up?" one girl asked.

"Thanks for asking, but no. We respect Orange Cat's right to decide what she wants. If she comes and rubs against your legs while you're sitting, she might end up in your lap," Willow instructed. "But remember, animals don't like screaming noises. It hurts their ears. They like soft, gentle touches from humans, never grabbing or yanking. They are nature's creatures, so we take care not to hurt them."

While Orange Cat was rubbing against Tracy's legs, her neighbor, Margaret, asked, "Are these your parents?"

Laurel answered, "Yes. Tracy's our daughter and Willow is her sister. She's been a member of our family since she was four years old."

"It's so nice to meet you. Tracy is such a patient young lady," the woman said, looking directly into Laurel's eyes. "She never complains."

Laurel understood the woman's warning and put her arm around Tracy's shoulder. "I hope she's not too patient. Women nowadays need to speak up. I'm in favor of equal rights for all. How about you?" Laurel asked the woman.

"Absolutely, it's a new day. I'm raising two girls and they better not let anyone mistreat them at work or at home," she said. "This is Lily, and this is Ruth."

Tracy whispered in Laurel's ear, "Can I call you, Mom?"

Laurel whispered back. "I'd be honored. Brian and I have been hoping you would call us Mom and Dad. We love you very much."

"The only Dad I ever knew was Brian," Tracy whispered. "Do you think Willow will mind?"

"I know she'd be pleased. She's been wanting to tell you to do that, but we told her to wait, thinking it might upset you," Laurel explained.

Orange Cat had waited long enough for Tracy's attention. She was now meowing loudly, her paws scratching on Tracy's knees. "Come here, Orange Cat," Tracy said, bending down to pick her up. She buried her head in the fur, to both snuggle and brush her tears away. When Tracy looked up, Brian was beside her, "This is my dad," she stated proudly.

Brian leaned over and kissed Tracy's cheek before saying, "Thank you. You honor me."

All of Roland's attention had been focused on his game of horseshoes, so Laurel decided to take advantage of the opportunity. "I'd like to see your trailer," she asked. "Your dad and I are thinking about buying an RV, so when I retire, we can take trips to the National Parks."

Tracy's concern over Roland's reaction made her miss the significance of why Laurel wanted to see the trailer. Tracy saw he wasn't watching but still hesitated. "Roland doesn't let me pick up his things. He hasn't had a chance to do that this week," she answered.

"We don't care," Laurel assured her. "Orange Cat needs a drink of water, and I want to feel the energy in your home." She put her arm around Tracy's shoulder and led her toward the row of trailers. "Remember how Grandma said that a home absorbs the energy of the family? You can feel it as soon as you enter."

"You might not like mine," Tracy admitted. "It's the red one, right there."

Orange Cat seemed to sense Tracy's fear, so she changed position, putting two legs around Tracy's neck, and purring in her ear. Tracy laughed, opened the door to her trailer, and announced, "Come on in."

Laurel went in first, followed by Brian, Willow and finally Tracy and Orange Cat. "I'll get Orange Cat some water," Tracy said, as she walked past them toward the sink. It was filled with empty beer cans.

Willow counted at least six before offering, "Let me help you. I'll get these out of the way. Where do you want them?"

Tracy handed Willow a box of garbage bags and apologized, "I'm sorry it's a mess."

Laurel was holding out her hands like Grandma did when she was scanning the energy of a new place. "I can't feel your energy," she admitted. "Where's your happy joy?"

Tracy nudged Willow to take Orange Cat and then said, "My things are in this drawer." She led them to the back of the trailer, where the bed was neatly made. She opened her drawer and, being more polite than nosy, they all looked inside at the neatly rolled garments.

"There you are," Laurel announced. "You were always the neatest one in our family."

Willow remembered Tracy treating the things in their home with loving care. Even as a young child, she never ran through the house or jumped on the sofa. When Tracy returned Willow's clothes, she'd check for spots, hang them up or put them in the laundry. Willow wondered how much of Tracy's demeanor had been shaped out of fear of her father.

Willow turned and looked around the trailer for loving touches, souvenirs or Tracy's things. All she saw were examples of Roland's disrespect toward Tracy. Sports magazines were piled in one corner, three shoes were laying on the floor, a pair of his dirty underwear was draped on the sofa. She felt a wave of resentment that forced her to leave the place. As Willow came down the steps, Roland approached.

"Hey you!" he yelled, despite the crowd around him. "I told you never to go in my house. You are not allowed."

Willow felt her mother behind her and stepped aside. Laurel walked down the steps, waiting for Roland to come to her. He was stunned to see her, and when Brian stepped out from the trailer, Roland's jaw clenched. He looked up and saw Tracy clutching Orange Cat while standing in the doorway.

"Why are you here?" Roland asked. "You can't go in my house without my permission and what is that stinking thing in Tracy's arms?" The crowd around him hummed with disapproval as they moved away.

Laurel stepped forward, announcing, "We are Tracy's family and have every right to visit her home."

"I'm her only family," Roland said, gritting his teeth. "Her parents are both dead. You have no rights. Who do you think you are?"

Laurel moved close to him, and without thinking, Roland backed up. She spoke softly, a few inches from his face, "I am Tracy's mother, and I am a Lenape Indian. We protect and nurture our own. Tracy has been in our family since she was four years old. My mother, her grandma, loved and cared for her with permission from her parents. Tracy's mother told us to keep her safe and protect her from harm. You are not a family. You are just a man who is living with my daughter, and if you treat her with the disrespect that you treat your things and her family, I doubt she will be here long."

After one last withering glare, Laurel went to Tracy and held out her arms for Orange Cat. Tracy walked down from the trailer and gave Orange Cat back to Laurel. "I'm sorry Roland acted this way," she said softly.

"He is who he is," Laurel said. "Nothing you say or do will change or control him. You can only control yourself and your own actions. Spend time at your sit-tree. Think about what kind of man you want to share your life with. Is it really one like that?" Laurel kissed her and walked away. Willow and Brian waved *goodbye* to Tracy before walking away.

They went back to Willow's house, sitting down around the table. They watched in silence as Orange Cat drank water from a bowl on the floor.

"You were magnificent," Brian finally said. "It was as if Grandma had taken over your body."

"You shook the applecart," Willow agreed. "What do think is going to happen next?"

"Tracy is mulling it over. I would predict that she left when we did. She's learned to run whenever the man in her life gets angry. She'll end up thinking at her sit-tree. She may even spend the night."

"Do you think so?" Willow asked. "What should I do?"

"What's your first impulse?" Laurel asked.

"I want to find her and be there for her," Willow answered.

"Good," Laurel said. "Get your backpack and put in snacks, water, and a blanket. Bring your mace. You know how to find Tracy. We'll let Roland see you leaving with us in our car. He'll be out looking for her and watching your trailer. We'll drop you off by the tree line. You know how to find her."

"Of course," Willow said. "Our secret whistle."

As predicted, Roland watched as their car drove down from Willow's trailer. He scowled at Willow when he saw her in the backseat. A half mile down the main road, they let Willow out. They watched her run into the thick brush. With the windows down, they heard her first whistle. They waited, listened to another one from Willow and finally the answering whistle from Tracy. Then they drove away.

Willow whistled again, and Tracy answered. They were close to each other, but still out of sight. Suddenly, Willow heard someone's unfamiliar footsteps in the brush. She looked for cover, finding it underneath a thick bush. As the steps drew near, Willow held her breath. They grew closer, then passed a few feet from where she hid. As the intruder walked past, Willow looked out of the bush and saw it was Tracy. She was stomping through as if angry with the world. Willow whistled, and Tracy turned around.

When Willow climbed out from cover, Tracy ran to her arms. It felt like they were reenacting their game of hide-and-seek, except now they had real-life problems from which they could no longer hide.

"How dare he treat my family that way, and in front of everyone," Tracy began.

"I've never seen you mad before," Willow admitted. "Good for you. Where do you want to go?"

"Let's go down by the stream. I found a great place to sit the last time I ran away," Tracy admitted. "Roland won't go looking for me. He's a real towny. He's never hiked or even taken a walk around the property. At night, he gets spooked by the bats catching bugs. He'll be inside in a few minutes, sulking on the sofa."

"I'm here to support you," Willow said. "I don't care what Roland's doing. Do you?"

"Yes and no," Tracy admitted. "I'm not sure."

"Let's talk about something else," Willow suggested, when they arrived at the sitting place. "Why don't you eat a sandwich? I have a doozy of a story to tell you about Grandma and how you came to be in our family. I just heard it today, and that's not all. Wait till you hear why our family talks the way they do."

The crickets chirped, and an owl swooped down to inspect the humans in its turf. When Willow had shared all the new information, they laid back and looked up at the stars.

"Remember how Grandma would have us camp out in her woods?" Tracy asked. "Why haven't we done this before?"

"We were too busy trying to act like grown-ups," Willow suggested.

"Isn't that what we're supposed to do?" Tracy asked.

"Not me," Willow announced. "I have no intention of following the standard pattern for our lives."

"Why not?" Tracy asked. "I thought we were going to get married, have kids that would play with each other and all that?"

"All what?" Willow asked. "Are you kidding? Aren't you curious to see what goes on in other towns, states, countries? I have a different plan for my life. You can come along if you want, but you're in charge of your own life. Only you can decide what you want to do."

"What's your plan?" Tracy asked.

"I thought we were going to spend the weekends vending at different music festivals. I've even thought about quitting our jobs and following some bands around full-time during the summer. Grandma's tent and gear should work for both of us. We can live off what we make selling things. If we don't do it now, then when?"

"After summer, what would we do?" Tracy asked.

"We could rent a house, and get a job at another hospital in a different town. You wanted to take a course in massage, and so do I."

Tracy said, "I still do. I think it would be a good way to set up my own hours when I have children. I want to stay home with them as much as possible, so I can teach them everything Grandma taught us."

"I want to set up my own studio, so I can control my schedule, support myself and travel as many places as I can afford," Willow said.

"You were always the curious one," Tracy suggested. "I have to think about it."

"Don't tell Roland, no matter what sweet nothings he says in your ear," Willow insisted.

"I promise," Tracy agreed. "If I know Roland, he's back home thinking of all kinds of ways to make up to me. He really loves me."

Ten

They had talked for over two hours, enjoying the chance to have an uninterrupted, honest conversation. As they walked back, Willow said, "I'm so sorry about your parents. I didn't know."

"I don't think about their deaths; I just can't," Tracy admitted.

"I'm going to wait until you get in the trailer. If Roland starts yelling or acting out of control, just whistle," Willow instructed. "If I don't hear a whistle in ten minutes, I'll walk home. I'm coming down tomorrow morning to do my laundry and take a shower. Let me know how you're doing."

"Don't worry," Tracy insisted. "I'll whistle if I need help."

Willow listened carefully the next ten minutes, then walked home. When she saw the lights in Fern, she felt a wave of regret. *I'll miss this place. I better enjoy it while I can.* When she wrote in her journal that evening, her day's words of gratitude were: "secret whistle," "being Lenape" and "my sister, Tracy."

By 10:30 in the morning, Willow's clothes had been washed, folded and put in Bumper. She'd enjoyed a long shower, given her phone number to Margaret, and still, Tracy hadn't shown up. In one last attempt to stay close, she'd brought her yoga mat into the main room of the community center and was going through her routine.

Tracy came running in, her eyes wide with excitement, saying, "Willow, you'll never guess what!"

Willow's heart sank as she thought of the worst scenarios. *He asked her to marry him, or she's pregnant.* Willow sat cross-legged on the mat and looked up at Tracy.

Tracy plopped down on the other end of the mat, her legs crossing like Willow's. The mediation position calmed her. "Carla just talked to me. She saw me holding Orange Cat yesterday," she explained. "The farmer down the road called her. Someone dumped kittens in his field. He's going to drown them unless someone comes to get them. Roland said I can have one. He even suggested that you go with me to pick one out. Roland says the kitten will make us a real family. Come," she insisted, standing up and pulling her arm. "I saw Bumper outside."

Willow drove while Tracy hung her head out of the window, looking for the kittens. "Stop! The farmer must have put them in a box," she yelled, almost opening the door, as Willow pulled over and backed up. Tracy bolted, running as fast as she could. Willow paused, took her phone out, and put it on pictures. She snapped the first one as Tracy lifted an orange kitten from the box. The lighting was perfect for catching Tracy's euphoric mood as the little orange kitten looked up at her. As she walked closer, Willow kept snapping pictures: Tracy kissing the little thing, Tracy with tears of joy.

"I needed this kitten to fill the hole in my heart," Tracy confessed.

Willow felt a stab of sadness, as she comprehended the deep sorrow Tracy had hidden all these years. "Let me look at her," she said, holding out her hand.

"No, not yet," Tracy said, cuddling the kitten in a protective hug.

The movement shocked Willow. Tracy was the first one to offer Willow the plumpest peach, the best seat on the school bus, the warmest sweater. They'd spent their lives playing, *No, you,* back and forth. Then Willow saw what Tracy wanted. In the bottom of the box, a little puff of fur barely moved. "Pick it up," Tracy urged.

"I am not going to take a kitten home," Willow swore, as she picked up the little thing and put it on the ground. "I'm not even going to hold it, and don't you pressure me." Tracy wasn't listening, she was swooning over her kitten. Willow looked down and saw the puff-ball pull itself over to her foot. She stared down in amazement as the little thing struggled to put its paw on the toe of her sneaker. One of her grandma's sayings flashed through her memory, *Cat's choose us; we don't choose them.*

Willow leaned down and picked up the tiny creature. It was covered in fleas, thin and barely alive. "I'll nurse this one back to life, but I won't keep it," Willow insisted. "Let's go. I saw a vet's office close to the hospital."

"Are there more kittens?" Tracy asked. She looked back in the box and around the grass, seeming to wish for more. "No, just these two," she announced, looking up with a huge smile. "They're probably sisters."

Tracy used Willow's phone to send a picture to Roland. Then she called him to explain they were on the way to the veterinarian. Willow could hear his reaction on the other end. "I said you could get a cat, but I didn't say you could take it to a vet. I'm not spending money on a stupid cat. That's ridiculous," Roland demanded.

Tracy looked over at Willow to see if she heard. Willow stuck her finger down her throat as if gagging. Tracy smiled and returned to the conversation. "Willow's kitten is really sick. Ours is healthy. I'm keeping her company. I'll be home whenever I can."

"I won't be here. You'll be busy with Willow and the cats all day, so I'm going to the stock-car races. You're not the only one who gets to have fun," Roland stated. "I might go out with the boys to a bar after the races. You do your thing, and I'll do mine." He hung up.

Tracy looked at Willow with an expression of shock. Willow gagged again, and Tracy laughed.

As the vet examined the kittens, he said, "This one is strong. Look, she's eating on her own. Keep an eye on her, she'll still need tender loving care. Whose kitten is this one?"

"She's my little girl," Tracy stated, picking her up and gently hugging her.

"They're both infected with fleas. We'll need to dip them in a very gentle solution. They're probably a little over seven weeks old, barely old enough to leave their mother. I bet their mother was killed." Tracy's body reacted. Her knees buckled, but Willow caught her in time. "Are you okay?" the vet asked.

Tracy looked at him, tears in her eyes. She blinked and finally acknowledged, "My mother was killed."

"I'm sorry," the vet apologized. "I had no idea." Tracy kissed her kitten as a tear dropped from her cheeks. Wisely, he turned his attention to the little kitten left on the table. "This one is fragile." He turned it over on its back while he palpitated its stomach. Two green eyes stared up at Willow. "She'll need to be bottle fed," he continued. "Are you willing to do that?" he asked Willow.

"I'll nurse her back to health until she's strong enough to find a permanent home," Willow offered.

"I wouldn't suggest that," he advised. "Bottle-fed kittens get totally attached to their owners. You'll be her mom. Even if she survives, she'll be dependent on you. I've seen them die from separation anxiety even after they've grown strong. We try to give kittens like this as much time as possible with other kittens. They'll groom each other, eat together and remember they're a cat. Do you live close by?" he asked Tracy.

"We're sisters," Tracy announced. "We live very close. Sisters with sisters?" Tracy asked Willow.

Willow reached out and cupped the little kitten in her hands and asked, "How often should I fed her?"

"The first two days, bottle feed her five times," he explained. "We'll give you the formula. You'll have to dip your cat three times a day for four days. She has more fleas than your sister's kitten. The fleas should be gone by then, but you'll get fleas in your house," he warned. You can't use spray or poison to kill them. She's too weak. The smell will kill her."

"What do I do about the fleas?" Willow asked.

"Keep her in one room. Table salt kills fleas. Put it all over the floor. The fleas will eat it and die," the vet instructed. "Leave your kittens here, so we can dip them and give them their first feeding. We'll get the formula and food ready for you to take home. You two need to get other supplies like kitty litter," he suggested. "Don't rush back."

As Willow drove away, she told Tracy, "I need to stop at the hospital. It'll only take a minute."

"Do you keep money in your locker?" Tracy asked. "I'm worried we won't have enough to pay this bill."

"Don't worry about that. I've got us covered," Willow said, as she pulled into the public parking lot near the waiting room.

"Why are we going in here?" Tracy asked.

"I have to pee," Willow lied. "The public restroom is close by."

"This was a good idea," Tracy said, as she went in a booth.

Willow was finished, had washed her hands, and still, there was no movement or noise from Tracy's booth. Finally, she said, "I'm worried Roland might hurt your kitten."

"Is that why we're here?" Tracy asked.

"I'm worried he'll hurt you too," Willow added. "So are Mom and Dad."

"He's not a monster like my *father*. He's just a lost soul like me," Tracy said, as she flushed the commode and opened the door.

"You're not a lost soul," Willow said, hugging her. "You are my sister, and you deserve a kind, gentle man like Brian, who has always been a dad to you."

"Roland has a lot of the red flags on that chart, doesn't he?" Tracy asked.

"I felt the same way as you when I read it the first time. The more I reread it, the more I'm convinced he is an abusive man," Willow explained.

"I'm confused. What should I do?" Tracy asked.

"Why don't you ask our hospital counselor for advice?" Willow suggested. "She likes us."

"I could," Tracy admitted. "What would I do if I left him?"

"All four of us will move back home. Mom and Dad insist on it. I only have a one-month lease. I'm sure Carla and Jim will understand," Willow explained.

"All four of us?" Tracy asked.

"Two sisters, with two sisters," Willow explained.

Tracy smiled and shrugged, saying, "I do love him."

"If we move back home, Mom knows a woman named Dr. Flint. She's a psychologist. You can talk things over with her," Willow suggested. "Besides, can you imagine Orange Cat, if we bring these two home? She's always wanted to be a mom. Remember when we found her sitting on the nest of mice in the barn?"

They bought litter boxes, litter, and a few toys at the pet store. They went to the grocery store and bought a large box of salt for Willow's trailer floor.

"I'm glad Ginger's fleas are gone," Tracy said. "Roland would lose it if we brought fleas home."

Willow chose to avoid the obvious and focused on the name, "So you named your cat Ginger?"

"What's your cat's name?" Tracy asked.

"I have to wait and see," Willow explained.

"To see if she lives?" Tracy asked.

"No, to see who she is," Willow said, smiling. They pulled into the farm lane and saw Roland's truck.

"I hate to admit this," Tracy confessed, "but I was looking forward to him being gone for the day. I want to set up Ginger's litter box and bed. After a little bonding time, I was going to take her up to your trailer."

"You're always welcome," Willow said. "If you don't see us, just whistle. We might go for a walk in the woods."

Tracy lifted Ginger out of the box and closed the car door. Willow's cat moved around in the box, looking for her sister. Willow put her hand in, and the cat held on to one finger. She laughed, and lifted the kitten onto her lap, promising, "We'll be home soon. It's time for your feeding." The cat curled up in a ball on her lap and fell asleep.

Willow had never fed anything this little or this dependent on her. She took the bottle, filled it with formula, and put the nipple near the kitten's mouth. She pushed it away. Willow put some of the feeding solution on her finger, and the cat's little pink tongue licked it off. Willow quickly put the nipple in its mouth, and the kitten finished everything in the bottle. Willow lifted her up to look at her little belly, and she could see the difference. "We'll put some meat on those bones."

While the cat slept, Willow made her a bed out of an empty cereal box. The litter box was filled and put under the table. *Even if the mattress is up, she'll be able to use it*, Willow thought. She woke the cat and placed her in the litter, never expecting her to go. The kitten opened her green eyes, scratched around and squatted. "Good girl," Willow shouted, with so much enthusiasm that it startled both her and the kitten.

Willow lifted the tiny cat up and carried her out to Grandma's hammock. It was a warm day, perfect for a nap outside. She laid down, placing the kitten on her chest. "If you're going to be my girl," she said, "you have to get strong and healthy. I want you to grow up to be independent, adventurous, and eager to learn all you can. I'll introduce you to Orange Cat; she will love you. You'll grow up playing with Ginger, your sister. I'll protect you, best I can, but I want you to learn how to protect yourself. You'll learn to run fast, hide in the leaves, maybe climb little trees."

Willow closed her eyes, hearing the soft sounds from the little kitten. When she felt the little one moving, Willow let her go her own way. The kitten was crawling somewhere, and Willow was interested to see where. Sick as she was, the kitten pulled herself away from Willow's chest down her ribcage and up onto her stomach. Once there, she crawled into a little ball and fell sound asleep. Willow lifted her head carefully and looked at her. She had crawled to the only direct ray of warm sunshine.

"So there we have it," Willow said, out loud. "Your name is Miss Sunshine."

Eleven

While Miss Sunshine napped, Willow put away her clean laundry and spread the salt on the floor of the trailer. When she was done, she saw two green eyes watching her. "Are you ready for a trip to the forest?" Willow asked. "It's time you became a woods girl."

Willow added Miss Sunshine's bottle of formula to the equipment in her backpack. She carefully lifted the little critter and tucked her into a pocket on top of her bag. She watched Miss Sunshine spin slowly around until she molded a comfortable bed, nestled down and closed her eyes. Willow placed the backpack on her shoulders, and they both went exploring.

They'd only been gone for thirty minutes when Willow noticed the pile of rocks. She carefully lowered her backpack, lifted Miss Sunshine out, and sat cross-legged next to the collection. The kitten rubbed her face against Willow's. "What do you think about this?" Willow asked. "This is turning into a treasure hunt."

Willow lowered Miss Sunshine onto the grass and watched, as she cautiously tested the ground. "Go ahead," Willow urged. "You can look around." The kitten tapped a dry leaf and jumped away when it moved. "Maybe this is too much for you, right now." Willow laid her back down in the backpack.

As Willow's eyes scanned the pile of rocks, she decided, *whoever built this, didn't know a thing about rocks*. She spotted two large quartz rocks she could sell for twenty dollars apiece. Willow lifted them out and set them aside. As she did, she noticed another pile of hundreds of small, round rocks. *These look perfect for painting*, Willow thought, as she filled her pockets with the prettiest ones. With her pockets bulging, Willow lifted the backpack and headed back to the trailer.

As she neared the stream, she heard Tracy's whistle. She stopped and returned the whistle and told Miss Sunshine, "Looks like our sisters are coming for a visit after all. Let's meet them at the sit-tree." A small furry paw rubbed against the back of her neck.

Tracy smiled when they saw each other. "Is this your sit-tree?" Tracy asked. "It's beautiful here, and it looks like Grandma's." She sat next to the tree, took Ginger off her shoulders, and placed her on the newly green moss. "Did you name your sit-tree yet?"

Willow sat next to her, gently putting her kitten by her sister. "Look how much bigger Ginger is than Miss Sunshine," Willow remarked.

"You named your kitten?" Tracy asked. "Does she love the sunshine?"

"Absolutely, and she brings sunshine into my life, just like you did when we were little," Willow explained. "I didn't name this tree though. In fact, I never named a sit-tree. Grandma sent us out to find a specific sit-tree for you. Do you remember how particular she was about yours?"

"I thought Grandma invented a game. We spent days exploring and drawing maps. It was exciting and fun," Tracy said, smiling.

"How many times did you run and hide beside that sit-tree?" Willow asked. "I always wanted to know if it saved you from harm."

Tracy dropped her head, picked up her kitten, and kissed it. "I don't like to think about all those nights," she said softly. "There were so many. Finally, my mother came up with the phone-call system to warn me if my father was in a mood."

"I'm lucky Grandma stopped that day." Tracy looked up at Willow and asked, "Do you know why she stopped to help my mother?"

"Grandma didn't stop to save your mother," Willow said, gently. "She saw you, a little four-year-old girl, ducking punches at your head while kicking and pushing your father away from your mother. She saw a brave warrior defending her mom."

"Who, me?" Tracy asked. "I always ran away. I should have stayed and saved my mother. She'd still be alive if I'd stood up for her."

"Your mother told you to run, didn't she?" Willow reminded her. "She wanted you to be safe. She couldn't save herself, but she made sure you were safe."

"And now I'm living with an abusive liar," Tracy said with tears in her eyes. "I've been such a fool."

"Why did you ever start dating him?" Willow asked. "He was always a troublemaker."

"He was the only one, except for your parents, that said they were sorry to hear about my mother dying. It was in the paper, and so was my father's trial. Everyone in school talked behind my back and made me feel like garbage. You never noticed, because you never cared what other people thought. You never got caught up in the high school drama. You did your own thing, just like Grandma did."

"Why didn't you tell me?" Willow asked. "I could have been there for you."

"I didn't want to tell you because I didn't want you to treat me differently. I always felt safe with you. Besides you did so much for me already," Tracy admitted. "Now I'm getting you in the middle of my drama. Are you sure you want to hear this?"

"Of course," Willow said. "We are two peas in a pod. Your drama is my drama."

"Then Roland has both of us in crisis, but I need to tell you how he got us there," Tracy said shrugging. "He dropped out of high school when his parents kicked him out of their home. He warned that I would be told to move out after graduation. Roland was staying at the YMCA. He kept it a secret, just like I kept the secret about my father beating my mother. Roland knew my father was on trial for manslaughter, but still wanted to be with me. I had never met anyone else who lived with family shame. Roland said fate meant us to be together and he had loved me for years."

"If he always loved you, why didn't he ask you out before?" Willow asked.

"Roland said he didn't ask me out because I lived with a snooty family," Tracy explained.

"Snooty family?" Willow gasped. "Us?"

"I told him you weren't, but he said I'd find out sooner or later. He's a liar. I just didn't know how awful he was."

Tracy handed Willow a deposit slip from Roland's checkbook. "When I saw that poster, I knew Roland was like my father. Roland's mean, sneaky and violent. Today he made a mistake. He left a note that he got a ride with two of his friends to save gas money. His keys were next to the note. I took the keys, opened his truck door, and unlocked the glove compartment. He had forbidden me from ever going through the glovebox because it held his personal property. I found the checkbook, and my name is not on the account. My paycheck goes into that account, and I can't even write a check to get any money out of it. I've been tricked," Tracy admitted.

Willow stood up, placing her hands on her hips, but saying nothing.

Tracy looked up. "He doesn't make near what I make. He's a liar. He told me that a friend gave him those fancy wheel covers on his truck, but he wrote a check for *one hundred and fifty dollars* to that auto store down the road. That's not all, he's paying over *one hundred dollars a month* toward a credit card bill. The card must be maxed out because he started using the checkbook to pay for everything. He hasn't paid my car loan for at least two months."

"That's terrible," Willow agreed. "I better keep this deposit slip, so he doesn't see you have it. You'll need it to stop your checks from going into that account." Willow stuffed it in the coat pocket filled with stones.

"That's not the worst," Tracy said, looking directly in her eyes. "Three days ago, he wrote a check to a Peter Miller for one hundred and twenty dollars with a note that said *gun*. I searched the truck, and I found the loaded gun, under the front seat of his truck."

"You touched it? You could have gotten hurt handling a loaded gun," Willow yelled.

"Remember how Dad taught us how to shoot, load, and unload guns? I picked it up, saw the bullets, and unloaded it as Dad taught us. I found a box of shells and took them." She reached into her bag and took out the box. "Do you want to keep these too?"

"No," Willow said. "This is getting too serious." Willow took out her phone and showed her the picture of the chart in the bathroom. "Look at this. Did you read the bottom of the chart? It says you have to make a safety plan. You can't just walk up to Roland and tell him what you uncovered. That's how women get themselves killed. You've got to be smart about getting away from him," Willow warned.

"I realize that now. Roland says he'd rather die than live without me because I'm the only one who ever loved him. He's capable of hurting both you and me. He's punched me in the stomach and twisted my arm and threatened to do more."

Tracy took off her tee shirt and showed Willow the bruises on her shoulders, and pointed to her ribs saying, "Two have been broken. This is why I run. I'm living the same nightmare I had with my father," Tracy admitted. "I never wanted to get you in the middle of this."

"Roland hates me because I beat him in a race in eighth grade. He's an idiot who's had it in for me since then. We'll deal with him together," Willow suggested. "Do you have a plan?"

"Tomorrow is Sunday. I'm going to tell Roland I need to visit with your parents because it's one of their birthdays or something like that. I want to see if I can talk to Mom's friend, Dr. Flint. A psychologist can help me figure out a plan to get away. We could take the kittens with us to make sure they're safe," she added. "I remember him throwing a stone at a baby rabbit one night. When I was shocked, he told me he missed it on purpose. Why did I fall in love with him?"

"I don't think you fell in love with him. You fell in love with the idea of a family of your own," Willow guessed. "Call Mom on my phone. Tell her about your plan. See if she can arrange for you to meet with someone who knows the answers. I'll take these two and feed them in the trailer," Willow suggested.

Fifteen minutes later, Tracy came running to Willow, her face revealing fear. "Mom gave me Dr. Flint's number, and I called her. She wants us to go to our parents' house tonight. We're supposed to pack up the things we need to go to work on Monday and take whatever else we need. She suggested I leave a note for Roland saying that Dad is sick and we need to be with him."

Tracy's eyes were wide with fear, as she leaned toward Willow and explained, "Dr. Flint told me to check if his phone could see where I go. She took me through the steps, and she was right. He can pinpoint everywhere I go when I carry my phone. His phone is linked with mine, and he knows where I am right now, and he knew where I was in the woods."

Tracy's hands shot to her hips, her mouth drawn tight against her teeth.

She almost growled as she realized, "That creep knew where I was every time I ran into the woods. He didn't wait in the dark worrying about me. He knew when I was coming home and staged it like he'd been sorry for being so mean."

Tracy stopped talking and shook her head before adding, "He knew where I was and never came after me. If you hadn't met me that night in the woods, I'd have been sitting there alone all night. He never came to bring me home, and he must know where my sit-tree is too! I was never safe."

Tracy grabbed Willow's shoulders urging, "We've got to leave, and we're both to take the box of bullets and our cars. Dr. Flint says Roland will know everything has changed as soon as he sees me. We have to leave before that happens. She's right. I don't want to spend one more night under the same roof as that bully," Tracy said. "How long will it take you to pack?"

"That's what I was doing," Willow said. "If he knows where your sit-tree is, I better get the key I buried there, then I can help you pack. Do you need my help?"

"No, I'm supposed to leave as much as I can, so he doesn't suspect something right away," Tracy explained. "I'll leave the door open for him. I'll just get a few of my clothes and all of Ginger's things. She told me to drop my phone on the floor like it fell out on the way out the door. Let's go now. He could come home anytime."

Willow went to Tracy's sit-tree and noticed her mistake. She'd left a large white quartz stone under the tree, one she knew Tracy would love. *If Roland came here to check it out, he couldn't miss seeing the white rock,* she realized. Willow pushed the stone over and dug down for the key. She sighed in relief when her fingers felt the plastic container, but when she lifted it out, it was empty. *Roland has a key to my trailer*, she realized.

Willow went to Tracy's trailer, to tell her the news. They looked on his key ring, but it wasn't there. They searched his truck in the glove compartment and under the gun, but it wasn't there.

"We can't spend any more time looking. Roland could have hidden it, or have it on him. We've got to go now," Willow instructed. They pulled out of the farm lane, rushing to get away before Roland came home.

The ninety-minute drive seemed to take forever. When they pulled into their parents' driveway, a wave of relief came over them. Their dad was waiting on the porch signaling Tracy to pull her car around back and into the empty building where they'd kept Grandma's boxes. Tracy transferred her things into Bumper.

"Tracy, did you ever tell Roland where Grandma lived?" he asked. "Think hard. Did you point out where you would go to be with Grandma?"

"No, never," Tracy said with certainty. "Grandma didn't want people knowing where she lived. Only those she trusted. I thought it was our secret place."

"Good," he said. "Dr. Flint suggests we all leave and go somewhere Roland doesn't know about. If he comes by this house, he'll see the lights are off, and we're all gone. He'll believe there's been an emergency and we're off somewhere taking care of it. But if he finds the gun is unloaded, Dr. Flint says he could get violent."

"Where's Mom?" Willow asked.

"She went to Grandma's house. She packed things we might need and gave directions to Dr. Flint who'll be joining us there," he explained.

"I made a big mistake," Willow confessed to Tracy. "When I was driving to our parents' house, I remembered I'd left Roland's deposit slip in the pocket of my jacket. Now that Roland has my trailer keys, he may find it. Should I go back?" Willow asked.

"Never, it's not worth it. So what if Roland finds out?" Tracy asked. "We're safe at Grandma's house, and I wouldn't lose you for anything in the world. You have a heart of gold. You have always shared your parents, home, clothes, Grandma, and everything I hold near and dear."

"My family wants to adopt you," Willow blurted out. "We've wanted to for years. We want to make it legal that you're my sister, and they are your parents. You need a next of kin, and I need a sister. Would you like that?"

"I'd love it," Tracy shouted, placing her hands on her heart. "I'd love to be a real member of this family. When Grandma died, and you started saving to get your own place, I got scared."

"One time, when you were visiting your mom in the hospital, Grandma told me that *most women fall in love with the first man that shows up*. She wouldn't marry Grandpa until he proved himself. He proved that on the Appalachian Trail. Roland was *the first man to show up.* He took advantage of you when you were most vulnerable, but we're not vulnerable anymore. We're two sisters who'll stick together until the right men prove themselves worthy of us."

"I'm not as independent or as adventurous as you," Tracy admitted.

"I'm not as trusting or open-hearted as you," Willow added. "See, we balance each other."

Twelve

"Look how happy Orange Cat is," Tracy said. "Ginger's all over her and Miss Sunshine lets Orange Cat lick away her fleas. The kittens feel like I do every time I'm with the three of you—safe. Grandma and all of you were my safety net throughout my life."

Tracy looked down at her hands, took a deep breath, and confessed, "Willow and I are starting to talk about everything and why things happened. We all kept secrets thinking we were sparing each other. My secret was, *I always wished that you were really my family.* I felt guilty about that because I knew Mother tried as hard as she could, but my father made it impossible. Last night, Willow told me that you wanted to adopt me. Do you still want to after this trouble?"

"Of course. We always considered you our daughter," Laurel said.

Tears rose in Tracy's eyes. "It would mean more to me than you will ever know. I'm an adult, but I still yearn for roots, a place to come home to that's filled with love. A center for my world."

"You would complete our clan," Laurel said. "You're the piece that's been missing."

"Can I take your last name?" Tracy asked. "I don't want my father's name. I hated him."

"Of course," Brian said. "I'd love that, and someday I'll walk you to the altar."

"It'll take a lot for me to trust another man. I know Roland's going to come after me, and one of us could die," Tracy warned. "I'm going to continue therapy with Dr. Flint. I'll meet with her at her office every Thursday evening. When I figure things out, we can have fewer appointments."

"Good for you," Willow said. "I'm glad we're here at Grandma's house. It's like having her arms around us, keeping us safe."

"Your mother and I've been talking," Brian said. "There are two baseball games on TV tonight. When I was in the trailer, I saw Roland's Pittsburgh Pirate baseball cap. If that's his team, he'll be happy drinking beer and watching the games. He won't get suspicious until tomorrow. Let's get a good night's sleep."

"You two sleep in Grandma's big bed. We'll sleep in my old bedroom. Grandma put a queen size bed in there for us. I love looking out the windows of my old room," Laurel said.

"She likes to look at all her trophies," Brian joked. "You can't blame her. Your mom was as fast on her feet as you two."

"I love you all," Tracy admitted. "I'm grateful Grandma stopped that day."

The next day after lunch, Willow scooped up Miss Sunshine and took her down to Grandma's sit-tree. She held her gently as she extended the bottle of formula toward the kitten's mouth. Miss Sunshine opened wide, placing her two front paws on the bottle as she drank. "Good girl, eat it all up. A few more days on this formula and you'll catch up to your sister."

Willow placed her kitten on the grass. The sun showed fur growing, where flea bites had been. "Look at you! I see black, white, grey, and a little orange. You're going to be a calico cat. You're pretty," Willow said.

Her cell phone rang, and when she saw the number, the pleasant mood of the day was shattered. "Hello," Willow answered.

"Are you and Tracy in your trailer?" Margaret asked, in a panicked tone.

"No! We're with our parents. What's happened?" Willow asked.

"Roland's furious. One of the older boys told him that you and Tracy were going through his truck," Margaret warned. "Roland started yelling, unlocked the truck, and was in there for a few minutes. When he climbed out, he was holding a gun and saying curse words about you two. I took my girls inside and called you."

"I'll call Jim," Willow said. "He knows people on the police force. Thank you for letting us know." Willow hung up and dialed Jim. "Jim, it's Willow," she said. "Tracy and I left the farm yesterday, while Roland was gone. She's had enough of his abuse. You may have to call the police. Roland found out that Tracy and I took a box of bullets out of his truck and unloaded his gun. Margaret warned me that Roland's lost control and was yelling threats as he drove off toward my trailer. I think Roland realizes Tracy isn't coming back. He found Tracy's key to my trailer, so he might go in and trash my place."

"I'll call the police and let you know what happens," Jim promised before hanging up.

They sat around Grandma's table, tears welling in Tracy's eyes. "Why do I feel sorry for him?" she asked.

Laurel motioned to Brian, and they left the room for a few minutes. While they were gone, Willow asked, "Are those tears for him or for yourself?"

Tracy looked up and answered, "I thought I loved him. Maybe I still do? I thought he'd fill this hole in my heart. It sounds dramatic, but I wake up picturing my father beating my mother to death. My heart aches."

"You talked in your sleep last night," Willow informed her. "I could hear the pain in your voice. You've been through more than anyone deserves."

"I'll never trust another man. I'm done being hurt," Tracy declared.

"You *fell in love with the first man to show up,*" Willow said. "Grandma was right. I believe there are good men that we've never met. Let's concentrate on making the next five or ten years full of fun and adventure. Then, when you do meet *Mr. Right*, you won't have a hole in your heart. You'll have a smile on your face and great stories to tell him and those kids you want."

"Come with me, ladies," Laurel said as she entered the room. "Leave your phone with your dad. It's a sunny day. Take your kittens. I'll take Orange Cat. We're going for a hike in Grandma's woods. When Jim or the police call, your dad will get all the information. He knows where I'm taking you. He'll join us there. Willow, did you bring Grandma's quilt from the trailer?"

"Yes. I grabbed it at the last minute," Willow said. "I'll go get it."

The next two hours, they hiked deep into the woods. All three women carried their cats, draped safely on their shoulders.

"Where are we going?" Willow asked.

"We're almost there," Laurel said. "I want you two to go ahead of me. When you find the right place, whistle for me to come."

"Which way should we go?" Tracy asked.

"Let yourself become one with the forest. She will guide you," Laurel encouraged.

Willow and Tracy nodded, enjoying the mystical manner Laurel was speaking. "It's like being with Grandma," Tracy whispered to Willow.

"I think I remember this path," Willow said. "Both of us were around six years old. Grandma, Mom, and Dad made us hike here, right?"

"Now that you remind me, so do I. We were both tired and complaining, but Grandma said we had to walk. We couldn't be carried," Tracy said.

"Let's let her lead us," Willow suggested.

"Grandma?" Tracy asked. "Are we headed to the place Grandma died?"

"Yes, I think we are," Willow guessed. "Are you okay with all of this?"

"I am. I feel peaceful, loved, and protected. Do you?" Tracy asked.

Suddenly, they heard the rustle in the branches ahead of them. They stopped, standing as still as Grandma had taught them. A large brown bear broke through the brush and stopped, ten feet in front of them. The bear snorted, studied them, and then turned and disappeared in the woods. Only then, did they see two little cubs follow her."

They held each other's hand as they moved forward down a faint path. When Willow and Tracy saw the large boulders arranged in a circle, Willow whistled for Laurel.

"Do you remember where you are?" Laurel asked as she joined them.

"We think we hiked here when we were young," Tracy said. "Are we still on Grandma's land?"

"Yes and no," Laurel said. "Have a seat on a rock, drink some water, and look around this place."

In the center of the rock circle, a large firepit had been constructed surrounded by smaller stones. It looked as though it hadn't been used in years, but ashes still remained.

After a few minutes, Laurel stood up and spread Grandma's quilt on the ground near the firepit. She sat down, crossed legged, and waved for them to join her. Once they did, Laurel explained, "This circle of rocks was made by your Grandpa and Grandma. It was the first thing they built on the land. My dad told me how they rented a mule for one week. He and Grandma moved the large rocks using the mule and rope."

"What is this circle?" Willow asked. "Is this where Grandma spent her last hours?"

"Yes, but this is not her burial ground. Grandma and Grandpa's ashes were spread in the forest on the way to this place. This is our family ceremonial ground. Your dad and I were married here. This is the altar your dad wants to walk you to, Tracy. Someday, you may choose to be married here."

"But I'm not Lenape," Tracy said slowly.

"Yes, you are," Laurel said, smiling. "Grandma made you a member of our tribe and a Lenape the day you two hiked here."

Laurel walked to the ashes in the pit, took a handful and brought it to the two women. She dipped one finger into the ashes and drew a line down their noses. You are sisters; I am your mother," she said, as she drew the same line down her nose. "Grandma has made it so."

They sat in silence, feeling the power of the moment. The wind whistled through the trees. They closed their eyes and let it rush against their faces. The cats meowed softly, so they let them down from their shoulders onto the quilt. Orange Cat began licking the kittens.

"I said *yes* and *no* when you asked if this is Grandma's land. It was hers, but now it belongs to both of you," Laurel explained.

"What?" Tracy gasped. "Her forest is ours?"

"Yes, all one hundred and twenty acres of it," Laurel explained. "That's why Grandma never wanted anyone to know where she lived. People have been trying to break up this land to build housing developments for years. Her lawyer kept her name secret, so developers wouldn't be knocking on her door. Once you are legally adopted, Tracy, we can activate her will. Both of you will own this land. We can still keep your names private, so you won't be hounded by real estate people."

"How can we pay the taxes on this land?" Willow asked. "I'd feel terrible if we lost it."

"We have instructions for you two to sell twenty acres. That will cover both the taxes and insurance on the land for decades," Laurel explained. "She wanted you both to enjoy being young and free. Don't feel weighed down by this land or required to live on it eventually. It will take care of itself until you know what you want to do."

Orange Cat sat up, turned her head, and ran off into the woods. "There's a mother-bear with two cubs in the woods. We both saw them," Willow warned.

"How nice," Laurel said, "I'm glad you saw her."

"I'm coming in," Brian yelled. "Orange Cat greeted me." He walked in, then paused a moment to bow his head and close his eyes. When he opened them, he announced, "We have news."

They sat on Grandma's quilt. Brian had made a trip to Subway and brought hoagies for the humans and cat food for Ginger. Willow took out her kitten's bottle of food from her bag and began feeding Miss Sunshine.

"I apologize for the modern fare. Your mom wanted me to light a fire and for us to roast hot dogs. Once I spoke with Jim, I had to change the plan." The women sat stone-faced watching and waiting.

"Seems Roland spent eight months in jail for assault. He beat up his father, put him in the hospital with a broken arm, two broken ribs and bruises. They have a protection order that forbids him to come near them. He wreaked havoc on their home, broke furniture, dishes, windows and worse."

"What could be worse?" Laurel asked.

"He hung the family dog," Brian said, shaking his head. "He's been out on three years probation. He's not allowed to carry a gun or associate with any felons. The man he bought the gun from was a felon. Roland was headed for jail without any connection to you, Tracy."

"Is he in jail now?" she asked.

"Yes, he is, probably for years. He did go to your trailer, Willow. He opened the door with the key, slipped on something on the floor and banged his head really hard," Brian continued. "The police said it looks like salt. Did you pour that on your floor?"

"Yes, the veterinarian told me it would kill fleas," Willow admitted.

"I'll tell Jim to let the police know. They were confused. Once he hit his head, it made him even angrier. He felt the pockets of your coat and thought it held his bullets, but it just held rocks. He found his bank deposit slip in the same pocket. He was so enraged that he used the rocks to break the trailer windows, then broke some glasses and threw coffee grounds on the bed. He grabbed a knife from your drawer and went outside. The police arrived as he was shredding Grandma's hammock."

"Can it be fixed?" Willow asked, hopefully.

"No, it's destroyed, but vandalizing Grandma's hammock gave the police a reason to put him in jail, and that's when they found out about his past," Brian explained. "Grandma stopped him before he could go looking for us."

The drive back to the farm was done in silence. Each of them needed time to process how close they had come to real danger. When they stood together, staring at the trailer, it was difficult to imagine anyone's fury. The birds still sang, and the trees still shaded their heads. The shreds of Grandma's hammock waved in the breeze, like a victory flag.

Other neighbors were up to see what had happened. They expressed their concern and support. The women hugged Tracy, telling her how glad they were that she was free of Roland. Throughout it all, the four of them remained numb. It was as if they were encased in a protective bubble.

Thirteen

Jim and Carla had cleaned up the blood, rocks, and broken glass. They had stripped the bed, and Margaret was washing the bedding in the community building. The two sisters went to the sit-tree.

They sat with their backs against it, listening to the sound of the rushing stream. Finally, Tracy admitted, "I've always felt like that rock in the middle of a stream. It took all I had to keep my head above the water." They sat, not talking, watching the stream splash over the rocks. Ten minutes passed before Tracy said, "I should be sad about Roland, but I'm not. I'm relieved. Is that horrible?"

"No, I respect your honesty," Willow said.

"I feel like today I've been lifted out of the stream. I'm safe. I'm one of the rocks in our stone circle," Tracy said, laughing. "I'm happy."

"So am I," Willow agreed. "We're going to make this summer a celebration, but now we have to decide about our immediate future."

"I know," Tracy agreed. "Even if we quit our jobs to sell things at the music festivals, we have to give at least two weeks notice."

"I have to work close to Miss Sunshine, so I can feed her during my lunch break. I could feed Ginger too… they're both very young."

"I need to take care of my finances. I'll open an account tomorrow, so my paycheck goes there next Friday," Tracy decided.

"You'll need to borrow some money to open the account. I'll lend you five hundred dollars," Willow promised. "I'll take my bank card to the ATM today."

"You know I never borrow money," Tracy reminded her.

"You're good for it. I heard each of us owns fifty acres of forest land," Willow said, laughing.

Tracy turned and looked at her, shocked. "We do! How about that, but we can't tell anyone."

"I agree," Willow said. "Grandma trusted us to protect her forest. Let me help you get caught up on your bills, and then we'll support ourselves."

"Thanks, I should be able to pay you back in a few months," Tracy promised.

"Where do we want to live?" Willow asked. "How would you feel if we stayed on the farm for a few weeks, while we figure out our next move? You have a great support group here. I think Jim and Carla will let us put up Grandma's big tent so we can see what it's like to sleep on the ground night after night. Last year we only camped on the weekends in her small tent. We'll have the trailer as a backup if we get sick of roughing it. The festivals don't start for a month, so we have time to decide," Willow suggested.

"That's a great idea," Tracy agreed. "I'll call the bank and explain why my car payments weren't made and send in what's owed. Roland may have missed more than I know. We'll need my car to transport things to the festivals like we did last year," Tracy added.

"We'll keep Bumper in semi-retirement at Grandma's house," Willow agreed.

"The last two days have been a whirlwind," Tracy admitted. "You'd think I would be overwhelmed, but I'm not. It's like all the pieces of my life finally fit together. Are you sure you don't mind me calling your parents Mom and Dad?"

"Are you sure you don't mind me calling you, sister?" Willow asked.

"Every time you do, I feel blessed," Tracy assured her.

"That's how I feel when you call our parents Mom and Dad," Willow said. "Let's tell them our plan to use Grandma's tent. They're helping Jim and Carla put plastic over the broken windows. Jim's worried because it'll take a few days for the replacement glass to arrive."

"Maybe he'll be relieved that we want to set up Grandma's tent," Tracy suggested. "Do you think I have to pay one month's rent on the red trailer?"

"Did you sign the lease with Roland?" Willow asked.

"No, he rented it before he took me to see it. He warned me that if I didn't move in with him, he'd find someone else," Tracy snarled.

"A real smooth talker," Willow joked. "He knew how to push your buttons. Let's go back to Grandma's house to get her big tent."

It was after ten when the two women pulled their cars up to Fern. "I hate that long commute," Tracy complained. "How did you do that for three years?"

Miss Sunshine was sound asleep in her special box until Willow lifted her out of the car. She kissed her head before admitting, "The apartments in Carlisle rented for more than I wanted to pay. I was used to living with you, but couldn't imagine living with another woman. I don't have anything in common with most of them."

"I know what you mean," Tracy admitted, as she lifted Ginger out of her car. "Neither did I. Grandma raised us not to care about material things. If it wasn't alive, it had no value. We didn't watch

TV, care about fashion, use perfume or makeup. I've never walked in a pair of high heels."

"They make no sense to me," Willow said, laughing. "Let's put the tent up tomorrow. It might take us a while to remember how to do it."

"Good idea," Tracy agreed. "I'm exhausted. What do you have for snacks?"

"How does cinnamon toast sound?" Willow asked.

"Perfect. The last time I had that, Grandma made it," Tracy recalled.

"Do you have any food in your old trailer?" Willow asked as she opened the trailer door.

"Not much. I thought Roland was cheap, but I guess we were broke," Tracy said. "I made good money; I hate that man. He didn't buy many groceries, but he bought those ridiculous wheel covers."

"Maybe fancy wheel covers are important to men like high heels are to women? We're too practical for any of it to make sense to us," Willow answered. "Let's go to the grocery store on Friday. We have plenty to eat until then." She laid Miss Sunshine in the litter box, and the cat immediately did her business.

"Next," Tracy said, setting Ginger down. "You follow your little sister's example. We fed them four hours ago, they should be good for the night."

"Let's give them a snack after we eat ours," Willow suggested as she dropped bread in the toaster. "They've had a big day too."

"You like bottle feeding Miss Sunshine, don't you?" Tracy teased.

"I do," Willow admitted. "I'm crazy over this little kitten. I'm glad you talked me into getting her."

They both ate two slices of cinnamon bread and drank a glass of milk. They were feeding their cats when Willow said, "I've been thinking that maybe we didn't get along with the girls in high school because we had nothing in common with them. I don't think it was us. I think our high school was in a small town, where gossiping was the popular form of communication, and we refused to participate."

"I was one of their favorite topics. They were cruel," Tracy admitted.

"They are insignificant now," Willow announced. "They can't hurt you anymore."

"You're right. Now, all those bullies are insignificant," Tracy said.

"We liked all the vendors we met last year. We talked for hours after the crowd went home. We had everything in common and learned from each other. We'd talk about different festivals, bands, tricks for living on the road, what sells and what doesn't. I can't wait to see some of them again," Willow admitted. "What about you?"

"I'm so tired all I want to see is a bed," Tracy said, yawning.

Willow taught her how to convert the booth into a bed with a double mattress.

"This gives us plenty of room," Tracy said as she slipped under the covers. "The mattress is great. It'll make spending the night in a sleeping bag feel like roughing it."

"I can't wait to live in the tent," Willow announced. "I want to quit our jobs and become gypsies this summer. We can follow the bands from town to town. It'll be an adventure of a lifetime. I think Grandma would approve."

Tracy sat up and turned the light on. "You want to give our notice soon? Why?"

"When we were talking about all the fun we had on the road, I thought, *why shouldn't we*. I've saved for three years to rent a place, but I don't want one now. I want to travel. We can move back home with Mom and Dad while we use that money for supplies to make merchandise. We need to tie-dye shirts, make necklaces, paint rocks, and think of other things to sell. If we give our two weeks notice on Friday, we can spend more time making things and exploring our woods. We own 100 acres of forest that we haven't hiked. Let's take advantage of being young and free."

"Sounds exciting," Tracy agreed, "but I'm too exhausted to think straight. Let's talk tomorrow."

"Of course," Willow agreed. "Good night, Sis. I'm sorry I'm just so excited."

The next morning while at work, Willow received a message with an attachment from April Braden. It read, 'Call me today. Thought about you and your trailer in the woods. We have a Hula Hoop Dance artist in town for one week. She's teaching at my spa. She needs a place to set up camp so she can make hula hoops to fill all the orders she's getting. I wondered if she could stay on your land for a few days. She has her own tent.'

Willow opened the YouTube attachment, and her eyes grew wide. A young woman was rotating a hula hoop around her hips, chest, neck, shoulders, thighs, knees and ankles while music played. She threw the hoop over her head, caught it with her other hand, and continued her freestyle technical moves. It was fluid and beautiful.

Willow sent the message to Tracy and walked to her next patient. She'd finished drawing blood when Tracy called back.

"We could do that," Tracy stammered. "We were amazing hula hoopers when we were kids. Tell her, yes. Ask if we can go to a class tonight. You can get my leggings when you go home to feed the kittens."

Her name was Ava, and she talked nonstop from the time they met. She told the class that she was trained in dance, yoga, and gymnastics and had performed in three Broadway Shows and several videos. Now she was crossing the country as she taught hoop dancing in studios and gyms. When she got to California, she was opening her own studio.

Ava motioned the class to sit on the floor, turned on her CD player and *Get Your Groove On*, started playing. They all watched in awe as she performed an intricate hoop dance, ending by throwing two hoops high over her head, twirling before catching them and holding them high as she fell into a split. The class applauded then stood up, ready to learn.

Ava stood, lifted one hoop off the floor and began spinning it around her hips while she talked. "Hooping is a good way to exercise. I don't know about you, but I'd rather do this than sit-ups." The class laughed. "Hooping tones and strengthens the muscles in your waist. The adult hoops are larger and heavier, which makes it easy to keep up. Choose a hoop from the ones against the wall. I have them arranged by size to make it easier. Stand the hoop on the floor and pick the one that comes to your bellybutton."

The class returned with their hoops as instructed. "Lay your hoop on the floor and step in the middle. Reach down and lift it up to your waist, keeping your hands apart on each side. We are going to spin it now. If you are a righty, give it a good spin counter-clockwise. Lefty's, spin it clockwise." The class followed her instructions, and all the hoops dropped except for Tracy, Willow and three other women's. "We have some experienced hoopers," Ava acknowledged and smiled over at Willow and Tracy. "These two are hosting me for a week."

The three women spread out Grandma's tent. "Let's see how long it takes for us to put it up," Willow suggested. "We might take this with us when we vendor." A half -hour later, they were bringing in their sleeping bags. Ava went back to her van and came in holding strings of lights. "I have a long extension cord. Where can I plug it in?" she asked.

Willow showed her the outdoor plug and helped her bring the cord into the tent. Ava started draping the string of lights around the poles inside the tent, saying, "If you can get electricity, these lights make tents look magical." She plugged in the lights, and Grandma's tent looked like a fairyland. Willow and Tracy gasped at the transformation.

"I've been a vendor in my life," Ava continued. "Your merchandise has to be different, and very few brick-and-mortar stores sell adult hoops. If you demonstrate hooping while you sell, your biggest moneymaker will be hoops. If you post some videos on YouTube, you'll get a following and might even end up performing on stage."

Everything about Ava fascinated both Willow and Tracy. During the day, Ava spread out tubing and cut them depending on what size hoop she was making. She'd made fifty before she left to teach a class the next night. When Ava returned, she showed Willow and Tracy how to cut the tube for their own hoop, use a hairdryer to warm up the ends and insert the plastic connector.

They stayed up until twelve talking, while they helped her wrap the decorative tape around the hoops she had made during the day. Ava explained, "You have to buy tubing in 100 yard lots or longer, so people don't make their own. You can get the tubing at any lumber yard. I'll give you names where I order my tape, but you can pay a little more and get it at the local craft stores. Shop the sales and use coupons to save money."

While wrapping tape, Tracy told Ava how Roland had made a fool out of her. Ava comforted her, saying, "It's just a chapter in your life. Be honest—you learned a lot, didn't you?"

"Carla called me today. The police notified the car dealer who sold Roland the truck. The dealer is coming to pick it up on Thursday. Roland was behind in his payments too, and since he'll be in jail for years, they own it. They gave Carla the keys so I can get my things out of it," Tracy told Willow and Ava.

"Take off those wheel covers. If you don't, the dealer will. Do you know where he bought them?" Ava asked.

"I do," Tracy said. "I saw the name in his checkbook. It's the big auto store ten minutes from here."

"Tell them what happened. Ask for your money back and buy some cheap replacement covers. You'll have money to buy supplies for your hoops," Ava suggested.

"Good idea," Willow agreed. "What about all the stuff in his trailer?"

"Carla explained that the police consider it abandoned property. What we can't sell, we'll give back to the Salvation Army, including those ugly dishes," Tracy vowed.

The women enjoyed each other's company, and at the end of the week, Ava had taught them more than just hooping. Her adventurous nature had been contagious. They handed in their two-week notice on Friday and celebrated by taking Ava to the farm cookout where all three performed hula hoop dancing. Ava left on Saturday, but her influence changed their lives.

Fourteen

"Don't forget those hub caps," Ava reminded before pulling away. They stood waving until her car turned west onto the main road.

"Let's go get them," Tracy said. "We better bring a screwdriver."

When they parked beside the truck, a group of neighbors gathered, treating them more like celebrities than victims. "My kids won't stop talking about hula hoops. Do you know where I can get some?"

"You can get them in any toy department. The adult hoops have to be ordered online unless you put in an order," Willow explained.

"Where can I order one?" Margaret asked. "I want to do it with my girls."

"We're going to make them, and we can give a lesson to you and your daughters," Tracy suggested.

"Can we order one too?" several women asked.

"Of course, I'll put up a paper on the community bulletin board, with a tape measure. It will tell you how to measure the hoop size you need, then we'll make one in that size. We'll give you a discount and only charge twenty-five dollars. We plan to make them next week," Willow explained.

"When do we get our first lesson?" Margaret asked.

"We should have a few ready by Wednesday. How about seven, Wednesday night?" Tracy suggested, before kneeling beside the front wheel of the truck, reaching up to Willow for a screwdriver.

A teenage boy stopped Tracy, confessing, "I told Roland about you going through his truck. I feel bad. I'll take the wheel covers off. I'm studying auto mechanics in high school."

"Thank you," Tracy said, accepting his apology. "We don't want to scratch them. I need to get my money back from the auto store."

"I go to school with a kid named Frank. He works there on the weekends. I told him what happened. Tell Frank, Tom sent you," he said proudly. "It might help get your money back."

"We'll do that, Tom. I appreciate your help," Tracy said as she spotted Carla walking up to them.

"I got a call from Margaret. She says we can order hula hoops and get lessons from you. Sign me up. You two were amazing last night. I don't know if you realize what a difference you made."

"What do you mean?" Willow asked.

"We all knew Roland was violent, ready to snap over the slightest thing. After everything he did, Jim and I were afraid to rent to anyone else. On Friday, you showed up smiling, joyful, and dancing with hoops. You reminded us that we can't let someone like him get us down," Carla said, before hugging both of them.

"We enjoyed it, too. Ava was amazing. If it weren't for your farm, we wouldn't have spent time with her. You and Jim have created a beautiful place to live. You can't let Roland ruin it. We'll be sorry to leave," Tracy admitted.

"We'll miss both of you, but we understand. You're going to have a great summer. If I were young and single, I'd ask to come along," Carla teased.

"I know that I haven't given a full month's notice, but we're leaving in two weeks. I'll pay for the remaining weeks," Willow said.

"Make me a hula hoop, and we'll call it even," Carla suggested. "The two trailers will be rented as soon as we advertise them. We got advice from the police to ask for references and get the applicants' name and birth date so we can go online and check for police records. That should help us avoid any more problems."

"Thank you for being so understanding. We were going to check for my things in the red trailer. Want to go with us?" Tracy asked.

"Yes, maybe I can help," Carla offered.

Tracy opened the trailer door, looked at the chaos Roland had left and turned to Carla saying, "I don't want anything in there. I can feel his rage."

Carla stepped aside and helped Tracy down the steps saying, "Jim and I will box everything up and put it in the barn. If I find something of yours, I'll give it to you. The police said we have to wait for a few months before it is all considered abandoned merchandise, then we'll donate what we can't use."

Tracy thanked her, then turned her back on both the trailer and the memories. Tom put the wheel covers in her car, and the two sisters drove away.

When they arrived at the auto store, they asked for Frank, and a teenager came out from the storage room with a puzzled look on his face. They mentioned Tom had sent them, and he yelled for the manager explaining, "These are the two women from the farm—the ones that got taken by that creep who bought our spinners." They were fully reimbursed except for the twenty-five dollars they spent on replacements covers.

"This is turning into a great day," Tracy said when they got in her car. "Let's go to the lumber yard and get hula hoop supplies."

They stood in the plumbing section and studied the wall of tubing. Willow reached into her daypack and pulled out her notes reading, "Ava used 3/4-inch 100 psi PE tubing. A 100-foot roll will make around twenty-five beginner hoops."

Tracy pulled out her phone and started calculating, explaining, "We'll save over a dollar a foot if we buy the 400-foot roll. We'll have enough to make one hundred hoops. Can we sell that many?"

"We'll sell twice that many," Willow said with confidence. "Now we need to find the connectors."

Tracy's phone rang, and she answered it. "Hi Mom, Willow and I are in the lumber yard, buying supplies to make hula hoops. We're in an aisle by ourselves, so I'll put it on speaker phone. What's up?"

"Grandma's lawyer called. Copies of her Will are ready for us, and we need to sign your adoption papers. Can you both be down here by two o'clock? He wants to do it today, and said he'll explain why when we are all together."

"We can," Willow said. "This is wonderful news."

"Her lawyer sounds as mysterious as Grandma used to," Laurel added. "He wants you two to come dressed to go for a hike, and you're to bring Grandma's little tent. Bring the kittens, too. It sounds like Grandma wants you two to camp out on the land after he gives us copies of the Will."

"I'm changing my name to Wilson, and Grandma is taking us on another mysterious outing. I love my crazy new family," Tracy said into the speaker. They laughed, hung up the phone and finished shopping.

"Bring two pairs of socks," Willow teased as they packed for a hike.

"We must take care of our feet," Tracy laughed. "Why was Grandma so obsessed over our feet?"

"I don't know," Willow admitted. "She'd check them after each hike, and never let us go barefoot, or wear sandals or high heels."

"I miss her odd ways," Tracy confessed. "No one watched over us like Grandma."

On their way out of town, they stopped to post the hula hoop signup sheet and attached the tape measure. Three women signed up before they even got out the door.

They'd expected Grandma's lawyer to be an old man, but he looked like he was in his fifties. He shook everyone's hand, introduced his notary public, and motioned them to sit in the five chairs he had arranged in front of his desk. "The first order of the day is to get signatures on the adoption and change of name for Tracy. Your grandma gave me copies of all the documents. I just need each of your signatures."

He slid a thick legal document across the desk to Laurel first. The room was so quiet that they heard the scratch of the pen against the paper. The sound became familiar by the time Tracy completed her signature. The family stood up and embraced, the tears of joy anointing Tracy to the family.

Once the notary signed and pressed an embossed seal on the document, the lawyer motioned everyone to sit back down. "I will submit this to the judge and ask for a court date. It should be scheduled in a few weeks unless he has questions or concerns. You should all appear in court on that day."

Laurel shot a look at Brian, and he nodded before asking, "Why does the judge have to approve this?"

"Each State has its own laws on Adult Adoptions, but most accept four reasons to approve Adult Adoptions." He read them from a section of the adoption papers:

"First, a former foster child who was not being legally available for adoption and grew close to the foster family as a child may be adopted as an adult if he/she wishes.

"Second, a step-child who has grown fond of his/her step-parent may be adopted as an adult by the step-parent.

"Third, an adult adoptee after finding his/her birth family may choose to be adopted by his/her family of origin.

"Fourth, a way to create legal inheritance rights within a relationship.

"I believe Tracy qualifies for the first and last reason," the lawyer reasoned, "and then there is a third. Your grandma signed a legal document stating that Tracy became a member of your Lenape tribe when she was six years old. The ceremony took place at the family ceremonial ground fifteen years ago almost to the day. That's a coincidence, isn't it?"

"Very little in this family is a coincidence," Brian explained.

"But I wasn't a foster child," Tracy said. "The judge won't accept that."

"I believe he will," the lawyer continued. "I was given this document, which your mother and father signed when you were five." He handed Tracy four copies. "You can share it if you want."

Without hesitation, Tracy handed one to Laurel, Brian, and Willow. They read the document and looked up at Tracy.

Her eyes never left the paper. "You two signed this paper?" Tracy asked. "Why did mom give me up?"

"She didn't want to, but she had no choice," Laurel explained.

"Because of my father?" Tracy asked, still looking at the paper. "He signed this paper with an X," she sighed while tears ran down her cheeks.

When you went for your physical at the elementary school, you had bruises," Laurel answered. "They sent people from the county to check if you were safe. Your mother and father were home, and he threw them out of the house. He was violent."

"Why didn't you tell me?" Tracy asked as tears dropped on the paper.

"Your mother loved you more than anything in the world. We promised her that she would be your mom as long as she lived," Laurel said softly. "The county would let you visit if we could guarantee your safety."

"So, Grandma invented the sit-tree?" Tracy asked.

"No, we all have a sit-tree. Grandma just made sure yours was also a safe hiding place," Laurel said softly.

"Where's your sit-tree?" Tracy asked in an accusing tone.

"What tree did we sit under when I read you stories?" Laurel asked, smiling.

Tracy nodded and whispered, "The red-leaf maple on the side of the house."

"Then there is the legal inheritance," the lawyer interrupted, trying to change the subject. "Your grandma protected her legacy with Estate planning. You and Willow will inherit all her land and holdings. It is my understanding that your mom and dad helped her develop this plan."

"Why, Mom?" Willow asked. "You and dad should inherit it first."

"There's an old saying," her mom warned. "*Be careful what you ask for*. Grandma's inheritance is complicated. We like our simple life.

We bought ourselves a travel trailer, our home is paid off, and we both get good retirement. We don't want or need anything more. Grandma raised both of you so that you would know what to do with her legacy."

"Once the adoption is complete, you will both inherit one hundred and seventy-five acres of her forest land," the lawyer tried to continue.

"One hundred and seventy-five acres?" Willow said, standing up. "You said one hundred at the ceremonial grounds."

"I'm as surprised as you," Laurel admitted. "Grandma must have kept buying land. She was obsessed about saving the forests."

Tracy just sat still, looking at her father's X. "I could have taught him to read," she said, looking up. "Maybe he could have held a good job if he knew how to read."

Laurel moved into Willow's empty seat beside Tracy, so she could gently remove the paper from Tracy's hands. Laurel placed it on the desk. She looked in Tracy's eyes and explained, "When I signed the paper, I asked your mom if we could help him learn to read. Your mom told me that she had tried many times, but it always ended with your father taking his frustration out on her. Once he went to an adult education class, but his temper got him thrown out. You couldn't teach him if they couldn't, and your mom would never have let you try. She wouldn't let him beat you as he beat her."

"It's too much for Tracy and all of us to handle at one time," Brian decided. "What has to be done today?"

"I'm going to give each of you a copy of the Will. You can read it at your leisure. I must warn you that there is a section which talks about a sum of money that Tracy and Willow will inherit once they are twenty-five," the lawyer explained.

"I'm afraid to ask how much," Willow admitted.

"You are in for another shock," the lawyer warned.

"What is happening?" Willow stammered. "Grandma lived on the land. Where did all this money come from?"

"Your grandpa," Brian answered. "He came from a very wealthy family, but both of them were like your mom and me—they preferred the simple life. The money was just invested."

"How much?" Willow asked, still standing, her mouth drawn tight in frustration.

"It's still invested, so we won't know until you reach twenty-five," he said, looking away.

"How much is it worth right now?" Tracy asked, getting as upset as Willow.

"Five hundred thousand," the lawyer muttered.

"What?" Willow screamed. "What is happening?"

The lawyer handed Willow a small pouch. "Your grandma was one curious woman. I'm supposed to give you two this. She said you would know what to do with it."

Tracy stood up and walked over to Willow. They opened it together. Inside was a compass and a map with instructions. *Camp here tonight and stay past noon. Bring four dozen eggs, three pounds of bacon, four packages of gauze wrapping, and three tubes of antibiotic. Trust me. Love, Grandma.*

"Let's do what Grandma wanted. She'll tell us what to do with her money. Our legacy is the forest, not money," Tracy reminded.

Fifteen

"What time is it?" Willow asked as she spread out the map on the lawyer's desk. "Mom and Dad, do you know this part of Grandma's land?" The lawyer shrugged and sat down on his chair, looking amused.

They all studied the map, their mouths open but saying nothing. Finally, Laurel murmured, "I've never been there. I didn't know Grandma owned it. If this is the scale," she said, pointing to a marked section on the bottom of the map, "we need to measure how many miles you have to hike."

Willow took out her phone and activated her *measure* download. Using Grandma's key as her guide, she announced, "Each section is exactly one mile long marked with a dot, the compass points change slightly at each dot. According to the map, we only need to hike four miles," she announced. "Isn't Grandma's attention to detail amazing?"

"It's three o'clock, and a hike in woods without a trail will take at least an hour a mile. Why did we come here at two o'clock?" Brian demanded.

"Your grandma specified two o'clock. I have no idea why," the lawyer answered. "I guess you were right. Nothing is a coincidence in this family."

"She wants us to arrive at dusk, with just enough time to set up camp," Tracy decided. "We still have to stop at the grocery store for the things on the list."

"How are you going to hike with four dozen eggs?" the lawyer asked.

Willow and Tracy looked at each other and laughed before Tracy answered, "We'll crack them into a plastic jug as Grandma taught us. "I'm grabbing two Italian hoagies and a bag of chips while we're there. Grandma didn't raise any fools."

"Let's hurry, we've got to feed the kittens before we take them on the hike," Willow warned.

"Did she say they're taking kittens on the hike?" the lawyer asked.

"All the women in our family hike with their cats," Brian explained.

"Their grandma raised your daughters to be as *curious* as she is," the lawyer stammered.

"Thank you," Laurel answered. "She did a good job."

"That depends on your definition of *curious*," the notary said, as she shook her head and walked out of the room.

"It starts at Grandma's sit-tree. I'll use the compass while you watch the mile marker on your Fitbit. As soon as we hike one mile, stop so I can readjust our compass points," Willow instructed.

"I think I know where we're going," Tracy said when they arrived at the first mile. "We're going to meet her relatives; that's why she wants us to bring food."

"We met all her relatives, and they're too sensible to wait for us to hike in the woods just so they can eat scrambled eggs," Willow reminded her.

At the second mile marker, Willow had an idea. "I think she built a small cottage on the land, and she wants us to have food, so it feels like home."

"No, that can't be it," Tracy decided. "According to Mom and Dad, she didn't want us to live on the land until we had a chance to travel or do whatever we want. She wants us to wait until we're twenty-five."

"Maybe we're just supposed to use it as a cabin," Willow tried one more time.

"Sorry, Sis," Tracy continued. "She knows we would worry if bears or squatters would get inside."

"You're right," Willow admitted. "I was worried as soon as I thought about a cabin."

On the third mile, the terrain had them climbing up steep boulders, so they were positive they would find a waterfall. On the fourth, all they wanted was a level place with dirt to set up their tent because it was already dusk.

"We must have taken a wrong turn. It's nothing but rocks up here, so we can't use the tent," Tracy complained.

"Take out your flashlight. We might have missed it by a few feet. Look around for some dirt or grass," Willow suggested. "Look over there… what's that shadow?"

When Tracy flipped on her flashlight, the shadow became a tree with one large quartz rock sitting in the grass. "We're here," she announced as tears filled her eyes. "How did Grandma get that rock up here?"

They lit the lantern and lowered the kittens to the ground. The cats stretched, dug in the dirt and went to the bathroom. "Good idea," Willow said and headed off behind the tree. Tracy went behind a rock. "I can't see a thing," she shouted to Willow.

"Neither can I," Willow agreed as she came back to the kittens. "Let's set up this tent. I'm starving." Miss Sunshine ran up to greet Willow. "I'm so proud of our girls. Didn't they do well on the hike?"

"Ginger slept in my pack or perched on my shoulders and watched the birds and squirrels," Tracy agreed.

"Miss Sunshine did the same. They're two of a kind," Willow said. "I'm glad we got sisters."

"I'm glad that I'm your sister, and I finally know the truth. I thought about everything while I hiked. Grandma patterned her life to follow the laws of nature, and it simplified her decisions. If one living thing can't care for her young, another adopts them. Grandma did the same with me, and she raised us together, so we're two of a kind. I can't change anything in the past, but I can be grateful for what I have. No matter why we're here, I'm going to honor Grandma's wishes."

Once the tent was pitched, they climbed inside with all their stuff. Willow closed the flaps. "It's colder up here, so the eggs should be okay. Where's my hoagie?" she asked, sitting crossed legged while she searched for Miss Sunshine's formula.

Tracy opened Ginger's cat food and suggested, "It's time. You have to let Miss Sunshine eat solid food now. Here's your sandwich."

Willow took her hoagie, watched Ginger run to the paper plate of food, and she waited to see if Miss Sunshine would follow. The little calico cat had her two paws on Willow's leg, her eyes watching for her food. When Willow didn't get it, Miss Sunshine turned and ran over to the cat food on the plate. "I loved bottle feeding her," Willow complained.

"I know, but she needs solid food now. You can bottle feed or nurse your own kids one day," Tracy comforted.

"I don't think I want kids," Willow admitted. "I want to travel."

"Don't I know it," Tracy said, laughing. "Every other teenage girl had heartthrobs on their wall, but I get the sister with a map of the world. Other kids dreamed about boys, and you dreamed about seeing Cuba."

"I had a boyfriend," Willow reminded her. "It was exciting and pleasant, but it didn't last very long. When you travel, the thrill lasts forever."

"You're right," Tracy admitted. "I think I'll travel too. I'm afraid when Roland gets out of jail, he'll come after anyone I love. Even if I had children, they wouldn't be safe."

"But you always wanted children," Willow remembered. "People would give us dolls, and I'd throw mine on the floor. You'd lift it up tenderly, and add it to your pretend family. I never understood that whole doll thing."

"Neither did Grandma. She'd tell me, *'Put down the doll, we're off to the woods'*," Tracy remembered. "Wonder what our lives will look like when we're twenty-five."

"Who knows what's in our future," Willow said. "I don't even know what we're doing up on this rocky cliff." They both laughed. "Let's go to sleep, I'm exhausted."

When they woke, they flipped the tent door open, expecting some big surprise. All the sisters saw was a mountain, trees, shrubs, huge boulders and treacherous slippery rocks behind them, and more of the same on the trail they had climbed. "Is this Grandma's way of putting us between a rock and a hard place?" Willow joked.

"Funny, but too close to the truth. What do we do now?" Tracy asked. "It's still cold up here."

"Make bacon and eggs," Willow joked. "I'm not carrying that jar with four dozen eggs back down the hill, but first I need coffee. I heard a spring last night when I was peeing. I'll see if I can find it and get water. Why don't you look for firewood? At least we can stay warm and eat while we sit here till noon."

The fire was made and the coffee brewing when they turned their attention to making breakfast. Tracy suggested, "I'll start frying bacon."

"Do you have any idea how much food we're making?" Willow laughed. "What in the world was Grandma thinking?" The words had hardly gotten out of her mouth when she smelled a putrid odor from something lurking behind a rock. Her hand slipped down to the hunting knife strapped to her ankle.

"Do I smell coffee?" a deep voice asked. "Am I delirious?"

"I smell it too," another man answered, and a foot slipped down the large boulder a few feet away. Willow and Tracy watched as two filthy men climbed down the rocks on the mountain behind them. When they saw Willow and Tracy, they stopped and stared before asking, "Did you two camp here last night with those kittens?"

"Yes," Willow answered. "Why are you here?"

"Same reason as you, I guess," the other man said. "We're hiking the trail."

Willow turned to look at Tracy before saying, "Grandma had us camp on the Appalachian Trail."

"We're thru-hikers, so we stink," one man confessed, "but I'd sure appreciate a small cup of coffee. We'll stay downwind."

"What's a thru-hiker?" Tracy asked.

"Someone who starts at the beginning of a trail and walks the whole thing before they quit," one man explained as he handed over his tin cup. "We started in Maine and planned to hike all 2,200 miles to Georgia."

"Our Grandma and Grandpa did that," Willow bragged as she filled his cup with coffee. "She was one of the first women to thru-hike the trail."

"I'm impressed," he said, before taking a sip. "We were wondering if we could make it. We're out of water, and the rocks tore up our feet and ankles."

Willow smiled at Tracy before saying, "We have antibiotic cream and some gauze. There's a good spring a quarter mile in that direction. It's deep enough to soak your feet and wash off. You can do that while we make bacon and eggs."

"You two are lifesavers," the other man said. "I'm going to wash my other pair of socks too. Promise to save us some food."

"Don't worry, we have plenty," Tracy said as the bacon started to cook.

"As soon as the other hikers smell that bacon they'll be hurrying down the path," he said as he limped toward the stream.

"So now we know," Tracy said, once they left. "Grandma bought land next to the Appalachian Trail. She wanted us to know about it."

"She was always one for surprises," Willow said, reaching for the jar of eggs. "Why did she want us to wake up here?"

"Maybe because of the spring? The view isn't awe-inspiring. All I see is rocks," Tracy said. "Maybe I should climb up a few and look around while you cook."

"Good idea," Willow said. "Don't slip—use your poles."

Ten minutes later, Tracy came down the rocks urging, "Sis, you have to come with me. I can't explain it." The two men were walking back from the stream, so she yelled, "Eat whatever you want. I have to take my sister to see what's up this trail. Don't let our kittens try to follow. We don't have backpacks on yet."

The sun was up, illuminating the colors of nature. They climbed up two large boulders, stood on top and stared down hundreds of feet into a panoramic scene of a valley with a river running through and another mountain of forest land rising on the opposite side. "It's got to be the most beautiful place on earth," Tracy whispered.

"One of them," Willow suggested. "No wonder Grandma bought more land."

"Hello," someone yelled, and four more hikers headed their way. "Do we smell coffee and bacon?"

The flow of hikers continued throughout the day, each taking advantage of the stream, the food, and the medical supplies. Some rested for hours, enjoying the conversation of other hikers, some ate quickly trying to keep their schedule for the day. All of them were filled with gratitude toward Willow and Tracy. One asked, "Does this place have a name?"

Willow answered, "Yes, this is Nuhema's Landing. She wanted us to come here today with all this food to help hikers. She was one of the first women to be a thru-hiker on the trail."

It was after two when the food was gone, and they packed up all their gear. The sisters walked around, looking for level land, and checking out the stream. "This is a beautiful location," Tracy said.

"For what?" Willow asked. "We never had a chance to read her Will. I guess we have four years to figure out what she was trying to tell us, but now we better start back home."

"What is home, now?" Tracy asked as they started climbing down the steep rocks.

"What do you mean?" Willow asked.

"Is home at Mom and Dad's place, or is it at Grandma's?" Tracy continued.

"Now that I think about it, I don't want Grandma's things going back into a box in Mom and Dad's garage. If Mom lets one of us move into her old bedroom, why not live at Grandma's? It'll be private, we can make our crafts out of sight of neighbors. If we live there, we might understand what she wants us to do with her land."

"Let's go home," Tracy said, smiling.

Sixteen

They had two days to make twenty-one hula hoops for eleven women on the farm and ten coworkers. All of the women signed up for Wednesday's class in the farm's community room. The tight schedule kept Tracy from obsessing over their grandma's land.

Without any discussion, the sister's knew what role each would take to instruct the Wednesday hula-hoop class. Tracy did all the talking while Willow demonstrated and gave individual attention to those having trouble. When it ended, some were trying simple tricks while others were happy to keep the hoop up on their hips for ten or twelve spins.

All the members of the class were invited to perform with the group at the farm's Friday cookout. One hospital tech made an appointment to go through the red trailer with her husband. In all, it was a huge success.

"Ava said we could transport thirty-five hula hoops on the top of our cars," Willow reminded Tracy as they climbed into their sleeping bags after the class. "Let's keep making them until we move back home."

"We only have ten left, but I can transport them tomorrow night when I go to my counselor and stay overnight with Mom and Dad," Tracy said. "Join me so we can tell them together about everything that happened on Grandma's mountain."

"Thanks but not tomorrow. I'm going to take two yoga classes and say goodbye to April; then I'll run by the craft store to pick up more tape. I clipped out a coupon from a newspaper at work for fifty percent off the total price. I'll buy all the tape that looks good," Willow bragged.

"I've never seen you shop so much or use coupons. You're really into this vending thing, aren't you?"

"I can't wait, and I like making the stuff we'll sell. I'm going to enjoy every moment of this summer," Willow announced.

"I'm a little worried about money," Tracy admitted.

"That's because you always worried about money. No more," Willow reassured. "I promise that not only will we be able to support ourselves with what we sell, but we'll also be able to save money for when we go to massage school."

"Are we still going to massage school?" Tracy asked. "I wasn't sure after our trip to the lawyer's office."

Willow sat up, turned on the lantern, and stared at Tracy. "Didn't I tell you?"

Tracy sat up, cross-legged, and shook her head. "You get more like Grandma every day. I don't know what you're thinking or why. It's all a mystery to me," she said as she shrugged.

"Didn't we talk about Nuhema's Landing?" Willow said, shocked. "It was the name of Grandma's sit-tree. It means *grandma*."

"I heard that name when a hiker asked where he was, but I never heard it before. I thought you were kidding," Tracy said.

"I saw Nuhema's Landing, as clear as a bell," Willow said, getting excited. "I thought you saw it too. It's what Grandma hopes we'll build."

"We're building something?" Tracy asked. "What are we building?"

"If you agree to the plan," Willow explained, "we are building Nuhema's Landing, a massage studio, hiker's store, snack bar, and campsite complete with showers, and washing machines. We'll have to find a location close to where we camped but approachable by car. We'll have massage customers from local towns too."

"Can we afford this?" Tracy asked.

"Of course. We'll use the money we get when we're twenty-five. It's a perfect plan. The Trail is open from May to October. If you want, we can work those months, travel, or you can focus on your kids. We might choose to work all year if we get local customers from town. It's all flexible."

"Why do you think Grandma wanted this?" Tracy asked.

"Who else got a massage from the time they were ten?" Willow said, laughing. "Remember Gentle One, the largest female Lenape we ever saw? She came every five weeks. You, Mom, and I would get an hour massage in Grandma's healing room. We'd do our homework or visit with Grandma while we waited for our turn. She'd make us supper, and Dad was thrilled to buy fast food on his way home from work."

"Gentle One came because we both had growing pains," Tracy said. "We continued getting massages because we were in sports and Gentle One kept us from getting injured. Remember when you fell and bruised your knee two days before States? Everyone thought you wouldn't be able to run, but Gentle One came every night and worked on you for hours. You ran and won, because of her."

"Hot then cold and some fierce massage worked on that poor knee," Willow agreed. "That's when we both started talking about becoming massage therapists."

"It had nothing to do with Grandma's plan," Tracy suggested.

"I think it did," Willow said starting to wonder. "Grandma had a massage table in a room she called the healing room. Isn't that unusual?"

"The massage table fit right in with all Grandma's herbs and woodland specimens. Whatever happened to all her plants and the massage table?" Tracy worried.

"Ask Mom and Dad," Willow urged. "Ask them if Grandma wanted us to be massage therapists and ask them if they want to come Friday night for the cookout."

The next morning at work, as Tracy dressed into her uniform, she announced, "Our parents are getting a life of their own. They've joined a group for RV campers. Friday they have a dinner meeting so they won't be able to come to our cookout. Last night I ate in their new RV, and it's bigger than the red trailer was. It has two bedrooms. They named it Wilbur," Tracy said, laughing. "Wilbur is one handsome RV. I've never seen Mom and Dad so excited."

"Why Wilbur?" Willow asked astonished.

"Seems Mom always said that when she retired she was going to get a dog and name it Wilbur," Tracy answered. "Mom's gone and done it. She retired. They're bringing Wilbur next Thursday night to our campground—better warn Carla. They want to camp out and help us pack up while we're at work next Friday. They can fit all of our stuff in one of their bedrooms. We can all go together to the last cookout and leave on Saturday."

"I have so many questions," Willow admitted, her eyes wide. "Most important is, do they think Grandma wanted us to build Nuhema?"

"They thought about it awhile. Mom once asked Grandma why she never suggested we hike the Appalachian Trail. Grandma told her that she didn't want us to become lifelong thru-hikers. When I told her about the land, both Dad and Mom agree with you. Nuhema must have been her dream for us."

"How do you feel about it?" Willow questioned.

"All that money scares me, and I can't imagine running a business," Tracy said sighing.

"Why?" Willow asked.

"Truth?" Tracy asked.

"Be honest, Sis," Willow urged.

"I'm from the poor family that couldn't hold down a job," she admitted. "I'm no Dolly Parton."

"Dolly Parton?" Willow said, shocked. "You've read all her books, studied her life. Doesn't she inspire you?"

"She's my idol," Tracy admitted. "Dolly was poor but look what she did in her life. I don't know if I have the confidence to get involved in building a business."

"You need to be motivated and inspired," Willow said. "I've been making our schedule of music festivals, and we're going to concerts in Virginia. After it's over, we'll go to Pigeon Forge, Tennessee. We'll take time out from vending, stay in a real hotel room with a shower and pool, and go to Dollywood. You told me they have a museum about her life."

Tears came to Tracy's eyes, and her hands shot up to her heart as she whispered, "Yes, they do. Can we really go there?"

"Yes, we can," Willow promised, and the two sisters hugged.

The last week of work was a whirl of goodbyes, signing papers, gathering reference letters from their supervisors, and packing up.

When Wilbur pulled next to Fern, the reality of how all their lives were changing became very real.

The sisters had bought a bottle of champagne, a bucket of chicken, and a collapsible grill for their parents. They sat together in Grandma's tent, Ava's strings of white lights making it seem magical, and talked about Grandma. "She told me you two were her legacy, not just the forest," Laurel explained. "She poured all her knowledge into both of you and wanted you to educate the next generation about the Lenape love of nature. She knew the forest would keep you grounded, and you would both protect it."

After the farm cookout, they took down Grandma's tent, folded it up, and placed it in Wilbur. Willow and Tracy spent the night in Fern while their parents slept in their new RV. Saturday morning, they waved goodbye and left the farm behind. Monday they went to court, stood together, holding hands as the judge made Tracy's adoption a reality and her last name Wilson.

The sisters moved to Grandma's house, placing all her things back where they belonged. The three hundred tee shirts arrived at their parents' house, and they picked them up and took them to a laundromat. They were loading them into washing machines when Ashley Coons, one of the bullies from high school, walked in. She pushed her jogger stroller next to Tracy, flipped her French braid ponytail over her shoulder, and picked up her sleeping daughter.

"I thought that was you," she said, holding her groggy toddler on her hip. "I saw you through the window. I walk my little girl by here every day. It's amazing how many people can't afford a washing machine of their own and have to use dirty public ones. I see classmates in here all the time."

"What's your daughter's name?" Tracy asked. "She's adorable."

"This is Priscilla," Ashley said. "I stay home with her because my husband works and supports us. We saw in the newspaper that you got adopted by the Wilsons. None of us girls understand why a grown ass woman needs to be adopted. It's pathetic!"

Willow's hands drew into fists, her heartbeat racing in anger. She watched to see if Tracy needed her support. It became clear that she didn't.

Tracy turned toward Ashley and said, "I don't care what you and the girls think. I hope Priscilla doesn't get bullied like I did in school and you just did now. One day you'll grow up and come to me to apologize, but for now, you and the girls are irrelevant."

"What do you mean irrelevant?" Ashley said as she shoved her daughter back in the stroller, making the toddler respond with a defiant wail.

"Insignificant, unimportant, inconsequential, trivial," Tracy said, before turning her back to Ashley and pushing more tee shirts into another washing machine. She never looked back as Ashley Coons wheeled the screaming child out the door and down the street.

They hung the first fifty tee shirts on Grandma's clothesline, stepped back, and watched the multi-colored tie-dyed shirts billow in the breeze. "You never said a word about what happened in the laundromat," Tracy said.

"Nothing to say. You said it all," Willow laughed. "Have you been planning that? It was perfect. I'm so proud of you."

"I have been," Tracy admitted. "I've been thinking about it for months and wondered what Dolly would do. I'm glad I got that off my chest. I'm never going to let anyone put me down again."

"You do love Dolly Parton, don't you?" Willow said, smiling.

"I watch her YouTubes, read her books, and love her music. If she can do it, so can I," Tracy announced. "When are we going to apply to massage school, and how are we going to pay for it?"

"When we get back from touring, we could get a job at a hospital close to our massage school. I was thinking about working in a hospital in Harrisburg and applying for the night massage school in York. We could still live in Grandma's house. It'll be less of a commute than we did to Carlisle."

"I want to apply to the massage school before we leave. Otherwise, I'll overthink it while we're gone."

They stopped to watch their kittens walk into the woods. "Where are those two going?" Willow wondered.

"No telling," Tracy said. "There's no holding those two sisters back. They're just like us."

Seventeen

Emails had been going back and forth between the sisters and their high school teammate, Jay, who had become a well-known tattoo artist. To celebrate Tracy's adoption, their parents offered to pay Jay to tattoo both sisters, so everyone in the family had given input into the design. His final drawing of the tattoo was so perfect, it brought tears to their eyes. A woman was the trunk of the tree, her one arm extending up into a canopy of branches and leaves, her other arm reaching down to hold the hand of one little girl who was holding the hand of another. The little girls were supported by the root system beneath the woman-trunk.

"How long will it take?" Laurel asked.

"Around six hours each, so Jay can only do one a day. We flipped a coin to see who goes first, and Tracy won. I'll bring my computer so we can continue to work on our festival schedule and order more supplies while she's sitting there. Do you want to get Facebook updates?"

"No, we'll wait to see the finished product when you get back to Grandma's house. Would you give us permission to pull Wilbur into your forest so we can practice camping before our summer trip?" Brian asked.

"The forest belongs to all of us," Tracy urged. "Grandma would be happy to have you enjoy it."

"Tracy's right," Willow agreed. "We'd love it if you live here permanently. We could work together on projects like a big garden. Could you ever downsize to Wilbur full-time?"

"Ask us after the summer," Brian said, smiling. "We'd like to try living off the grid."

"You can do your laundry and take a shower or bath at Grandma's house, but I'm worried how you're going to get Wilbur into the woods."

"Your grandpa made a three-mile dirt road from behind the little barn into the forest. We're going to try driving the truck in first and see if it is cleared enough for Wilbur. I'll bring my chainsaw to cut any trees that may have fallen on the road. We can burn the wood in a campfire."

"What if part of the road washed away?" Willow asked.

"I'll see if I can get Bertha running. She's been sitting in the barn since Grandpa died. You two could use a little tractor for future projects," Brian suggested.

The girls looked at each other stunned. "We've never been in that old barn," Tracy stated. "We never knew about Bertha."

Tracy's shoulder had the leaves and branches, and the top of Grandma's arm completed when Willow received a FaceTime request from Ava in California. "What's up with you two?" she asked.

"Tracy's getting a tattoo and I'm going to get the same one tomorrow. Here's the drawing... do you like it?" Willow asked as she held her copy to the screen.

"Is that your Grandma as the trunk and the two little ones both of you?" Ava asked.

"Yes, Do you like it?" Tracy said without moving.

"I love it. I hope it's going to be big enough to see when you're on stage. Where's it going?" Ava asked.

"It'll start at our shoulder and run down to a few inches from our elbow. Jay's been working on her for over two hours, and Tracy's never flinched," Willow bragged. "I hope I'm as brave as she's been."

"It's probably harder for you to watch her get tattooed than to get one yourself. You're protective of your sister," Ava reminded Willow. "I was going to show the both of you something you need to get," Ava said. "I don't want Tracy to move, so maybe I should call back later."

"I need a twenty-minute break," Jay said. "And I want to call my wife, Morgan. The baby's due anytime now." He helped Tracy to her feet and handed her a bottle of water. "Drink the whole bottle and then go to the bathroom. We'll have another long session when I get back."

"How does it look?" Tracy asked as she turned so Ava could see it.

"It looks sore, very sore, but fantastic," Ava answered. "I'm sending you the link to my newest YouTube demonstration on fire hooping. I'm using a hoop with five wicks that I light and then do a routine. It brings the crowd to their feet. If you're performing at night, it's spectacular. You two are good enough to learn how to do it if you follow my instructions. You might get a few burns at first, but then you'll get the knack. Have you ordered lite up dance hula hoops? You'll have to use them if the band doesn't want fire hoops up on stage. Once your tattoos are healed, you've got to post a few videos on YouTube of the two of you performing. Use that when you apply to get into the music festivals."

"We never thought of that," Willow admitted. "We'll wait till we post a YouTube video so we can share the link in our application to perform at the festivals. One site is located at a quarry in Ohio. They hold week-long concerts throughout the summer. If they accept us as performers, our camping fee will be waived, and they'll give us a spot in the musicians' section. Once we're there, we can get invited to follow other bands. We'll just have to pay the vendor fee, but we can handle that."

"Sounds good to me. Call if you have any questions about working with the fire hoops and send me theYouTube links as you post them. Good luck. Can't wait to see them. Now go pee, Tracy," she said laughing as she hung up.

By the time Tracy sat back down, Willow was watching the YouTube for the fifth time. "We can do this," she decided. "We can order the wicks and just screw them onto one of our hoops. Then you light them one at a time and look how Ava moves the hoop around. It's mesmerizing at night. What do you think?"

"I think it's the sexiest thing I've ever seen," Jay said, watching with Tracy. "A woman twirling around with fire is hot."

Tracy leaned back in the chair and said to him, "Make my tattoo beautiful. Looks like I'm going to become a sexy fire hooper."

"I'll order the wicks for fire hooping and four hoops with lights inside. How many shirts have we tie-dyed?" Willow asked Tracy.

"All three hundred. I finished the last of them yesterday while you were painting rocks," Tracy explained.

"Do they look like what you've got on?" Jay asked.

"Yes, this is our most popular design. Do you want me to bring some to your shop tomorrow when you work on me?" Willow asked. "We'll give you a discount so you can make a profit if you sell them."

"I'll take fifty in a variety of sizes," he decided. "I'm setting up in a tattoo show next week if our little boy holds off till he's due."

"I'm so happy for you, Jay. You've always been one of the good guys. What's Morgan like?" Tracy asked.

"We met in art school, and she's the gifted one in the family. I got lucky when I married her. She values the same things I do. As a matter of fact, she'd love your tattoo. She's always painting trees, and streams and nature scenes. Our dream is to raise our kids surrounded by nature without all that plastic crap other kids have," Jay explained. "We are having one of those little houses on wheels built. If Morgan's feeling up to it, I'll ask her to stop by tomorrow. You three would hit it off."

Tracy's arm was swollen and sore. The tattoo area was smeared with salve and covered in bandages. They decided to wait until Willow got hers done before they showed their parents. "How do you care for it?" Laurel asked as she dished out a serving of her beef stew over egg noodles.

"I have to keep the bandage on for one day and be careful to keep it covered from the sun for at least a week. He says it will itch, but we can't scratch it. Just slap it to stop the itching," Tracy said as she tried to spoon up the noodles with her left hand. "We sold fifty tee shirts to Jay, so I ordered two hundred more. I enjoy dyeing those shirts."

"I'm glad, because I need to focus on making the leather and feather hair clips and hemp necklaces. I've got most of the small rocks painted already," Willow announced.

"I saw them in the healing room," Laurel said. "I'd have a hard time picking one. I love the turtle, owl, cat, bear cub. I guess all of them. Where did you learn how to paint like that?"

"From a library book," Willow answered. "Plus Grandma always had us drawing and working with paint in the craft room."

Morgan showed up near the end of Willow's session, her shoulders drawn back for balance and her two hands cradling her belly and the baby inside. Tracy stood up when Morgan reached out to her for help easing down into a chair. Morgan took a few breaths and said, "Thank you. You must be Tracy. How is your arm feeling today?"

Tracy showed her the healing tattoo. "What do you think?"

"It looks like my husband has made another masterpiece," Morgan said lightly running her fingers over the tattoo. She withdrew her hand and apologized saying, "I'm sorry. We just met, but I'm one of those touchy feely people. Do you mind?"

Tracy looked down into Morgan's green eyes, and sensed authenticity. Her short hair was a mass of reddish curls that did their own thing. The only makeup she wore was a soft pink lip gloss. "I don't mind at all," Tracy said. "I've heard so much about you from Jay."

"He's prejudice. The man's madly in love with me," she said laughing. "He loves my thin ankles," she added as she lifted one of her swollen legs.

"That's my girl," Jay said looking up to smile at his wife. "What do you think of Willow's? It's almost done."

"It's beautiful," Morgan declared. "How are you feeling, Willow? Does it hurt?"

"Not too much," Willow said. "I'm so thrilled to get it."

"Jay told me about the story behind it, and I think it's amazing. Oops, there he goes again," she said, laughing. "This little guy is going to be a runner like his daddy. Want to feel him, Tracy?" Morgan reached out and took Tracy's hand, laying it on her stomach. "He's kicking right there."

"I feel it! It's like a miracle, a baby inside of you, and soon he'll be in your arms. I'm envious," Tracy admitted.

"Do you want kids?" Morgan asked.

"Yes, I did want kids, but I'm getting over a bad relationship so now I don't know," Tracy explained.

"That Roland was a bad dude. I couldn't believe you dated him. I told you not to," Jay reminded Tracy.

"You did warn me," Tracy said. "I should have listened."

"I dated a few losers in my day, and so did Jay. It just makes you more grateful when you find the right one," Morgan reassured Tracy. "If you ever want to hold a baby, come over to our house. I don't have any sisters, and I could sure use some female company."

"I'd love that," Tracy assured her.

"We'll have all three of you over to our Grandma's house, it's surrounded by trees. You can paint while my sister bounces your baby on her knee," Willow suggested.

"We've never invited anyone over before because Grandma lived alone and liked her privacy, but she always liked you, Jay, and she would have loved Morgan. I'll give you the address. It's a thirty-minute drive, so you better wait until your son arrives. Do you have a name yet?" Tracy asked.

"Yes, Jay picked it out years ago. He tattoos the mythical Phoenix on many customers with an emotional wound. He says that the tattoo seems to give them a new attitude toward life. Our son will be named Phoenix and hopefully he will make a difference in the lives of those he meets," Morgan explained.

Their tattoos healed quickly and became their pride and joy. They shopped for tank tops to show them off and looked on the internet to find costumes to wear on stage. They ordered three matching outfits—each set with a tank top and matching leggings.

Morgan went into labor two days after their meeting. Jay called and said she wanted them to come to the hospital to visit. Morgan was smiling happily with a blue bundle in her arms when they arrived, only a little pink fist could be seen swinging in the air. They stopped still, took out their phones, and each took a picture. Morgan loosened the blanket and showed his little face, arms, and legs. He was perfect.

A week later, Phoenix lay in Laurel's arms while Brian started the music on cue. Morgan and Jay recorded the sisters as they performed their fire hula hoop dance in one of their new costumes. When it was uploaded and appeared on YouTube, they all clapped. They had what they needed to submit their applications.

Before they left, Jay went for a walk with Brian. Willow and Tracy invited Morgan to bring Phoenix to visit Grandma's sit-tree. It had recently rained, and the stream was running high, breaking in white waves over the rocks. "This is a sacred place," Morgan said. "I can feel positive energy."

"This was Grandma's sit-tree," Willow explained. "Her spirit radiated love."

"I'm an artist. I think visually," Morgan said. "What did she look like?"

"Grandma had gray hair and big brown-eyes, and when she told us a story, her dark eyebrows would go up and down," Tracy said, smiling. "She was short, like Willow and me, and thin because she hiked through her forest. She always smelled like honeysuckle or flour."

Willow nodded and added, "Grandma always wore a long cotton skirt, hiking boots, and one of the tee shirts we'd give her for Christmas—ones with trees, ferns, waterfalls or cliffs. She never wanted words on them, just nature scenes."

"Around her neck, Grandma always wore a rock she'd found, then wove into a hemp necklace, and a hunting knife strapped to her ankle," Tracy added.

"Grandma was filled with love, but if she saw injustice, she could be a warrior," Willow explained.

"She saved me," Tracy said. "I doubt that I would be alive today without Grandma."

Eighteen

A few weeks later, their mom and dad welcomed them home from their first festival of the year.

"It was the best four days of our lives," Willow said, as they got out of their car in front of Grandma's house. "We had watched videos of Nelson Ledges Quarry, but they didn't prepare us for how much fun we were going to have. It was like entering a world where everyone enjoyed the same things. We jumped off stone cliffs into the spring-water in the quarry. Music was performed on stage, around the campfires, in the forest, at the beach, and on the cliffs. The songs connected us to each other, and we'd dance whenever and wherever we wanted. All the items being sold were either food or hand-made originals. I loved every minute there," Willow said, in more words than her usual brief exchanges.

"How did the cats do?" Laurel asked. "We were worried they might get lost."

"They were great. Once we showed the cats where our tent was, they took off and explored. Miss Sunshine takes the lead when Orange Cat is not around. She's not afraid of anything. I borrowed a kayak, and Miss Sunshine and I paddled around the quarry for over two hours. She loved it."

"Did you enjoy yourself, Tracy?" Laurel asked. "I know you worried about the trip."

"I did enjoy it. I was worried about money, but Grandma was right. Remember how she told us, '*Worrying is a wasted emotion'?*" We sold everything we brought with us, except for a few rocks. The people liked the painted rocks but preferred to paint their own. When we go back, we're going to bring paints so they can buy a rock and paint it themselves at our booth," Tracy said. "The Ledges is like the National Parks—everyone is careful to leave the forest the way they found it, rocks and all. We sold out of hula hoops after the first concert. We took orders from people who'll be attending the next quarry festival, but we can't transport more than thirty-five in my car. We might have to rent or buy a small trailer."

"Why don't you take my van?" Laurel said. "We won't be using it for the rest of the summer. Would that help?"

"Yes, do you mind?" Willow answered.

"Of course not," Brian answered. "We don't need it now. You'll see why when you get to our campsite. We were hoping you'd just pull your car up to our place before you unpack. We have a surprise to show you. If we take out the vendor tables, and a few other things, your mom, Orange Cat and I can ride in the backseat."

"Can we take a shower first?" Tracy asked. "It's been a long, hot ride and the cats need some water."

"Don't take a shower. You'll like what we found," Laurel insisted.

"You give water to the cats and grab some more cat food, while your mom and I clear out the backseat. Orange Cat is already grooming them," Brian said, laughing.

Tracy and Willow looked at each other and laughed. "You two get more like Grandma every day."

"I got Bertha up and running again, so I smoothed out the road," Brian explained as they drove toward their trailer. "She's parked by Wilbur. You'll see why when you get there. We needed to fix the road so I can keep our propane tank filled and carry in supplies."

"I've never heard you so excited, Dad," Willow admitted. "You've been having a good time, haven't you?"

"Both of us feel ten years younger. We love it here," Laurel said. "Look how beautiful the forest is with the sun shining down through the trees. If we had a few sheep, they could eat the vines that are suffocating some of the trees. They eat poison ivy and oak too," she added.

"The bears might eat them," Willow spurted out.

"We could put them in the barn at night," her dad suggested.

Tracy and Willow looked at each other in quiet amazement. Everything about their parents seemed to have shifted. They seemed more in love, holding hands and whispering to each other in the backseat like teenagers.

Bertha was smaller than they had expected, the front blade just a yard wide. They got out of the car, the cats running after Orange Cat into the forest. "Go change into your swimsuits in Wilbur, then we'll follow the cats," Laurel suggested. "Your dad and I already have ours on."

The aroma of their mother's crockpot, chicken-corn soup greeted them at the door. Her cornbread muffins were covered with plastic wrap to keep them fresh, but once they looked around, the food was forgotten. The trailer had changed as much as their parents. A vase filled with wildflowers sat in the middle of their table. Their parent's favorite things from home were inside, including a few family photos, the quilt Grandma had made them, the braided rag-rug she had woven, and the bowl Grandma had thrown on her wheel. The small chair Grandpa had carved sat in their bedroom.

"They've moved in," Tracy said hugging Willow. "I think they're staying here with us."

"Don't get your hopes up," Willow said. "We don't want to put any pressure on them or make them feel obligated to help us take care of all this land."

"I know, but it looks like they might be thinking about it," Tracy said. "Let's get changed and see what happens."

When they walked out of the trailer, they found their parents laying down together in a hammock they'd hung from two trees a few feet from Wilbur. The hammock was identical to the one Roland had torn apart. The sisters stood still, unable to believe their eyes.

"We found a box with our names on it in the barn. Grandpa must have bought this hammock for us when he gave one to Grandma. Can you believe our luck?" Laurel said, as she carefully stood up.

"How did he know how much this would mean to all of us?" Willow asked, running her hand over the hammock.

"He was as special as Grandma, and when he saw how we all loved swinging in hers, he must have bought one for us," Laurel suggested. "Grandpa had lots of money, but he wouldn't spend it on stuff. He invested it in land and keepsakes, like our hammock."

"There are two more hammocks like this with your names on it. The writing was Grandma's so she must have bought them for each of you," Brian added. "She never gave us our hammock. We think she wanted us to get it once you inherited this land. It might have been her way of telling us to enjoy it with you."

"Come here, you two," Laurel asked as she opened her arms to them. They all hugged, and then Laurel walked while saying, "When I was a little girl, this was my favorite place to come in the woods.

That's why Grandpa made a road up here. He built me that tree-fort," she said, pointing to a few rotten boards in a big maple tree. "You two liked the stream by Grandma's sit-tree. I never wanted to take you away from her favorite place because it was easier for her to watch you there. The stream up here is swifter. Come see."

"I was never allowed to go past this stream," Laurel said, as they approached the fast-running water. Our land ended where the white marks are on that tree. When we were at the lawyer's office, we found out Grandma had bought more land, remember?"

"Yes, how could we forget?" Willow asked.

"She bought the mountain that connects to the Appalachian Trail and the stream that flows down from it into a magnificent lake one mile from here," Laurel explained as they followed her through the brush and trees. "We'd like your permission for your dad to use Bertha to make us a safer path, so we can swim in the lake at night and look up at the stars and the moon."

"You two swim at night?" Willow asked.

"We do," Brian said as he walked behind them. "You should join us. It's a different experience at night. The bats dive in the water, the toads sing on the banks, and animals come to the shoreline to drink."

"Is it safe to swim at night?" Tracy asked.

"As safe as jumping off the cliffs of the quarry you went to," Brian teased. "We'd be safer sitting in our recliners in our old house, but we wouldn't feel as alive as we do here."

"Your old house? Does that mean you want to live here permanently?" Willow asked.

"At least in the summer and fall. We're thinking we might pull Wilbur down south to visit a few National Parks when it's winter," Brian explained. "We'll become one of those snowbirds."

"Would you sell your old house?" Tracy asked as they all continued hiking through the thick of the forest.

"Yes, I have no interest in spending all my time taking care of an acre of lawn and that big old house, and your mom doesn't need to clean it anymore," Brian explained. "We can help you two take care of this land. We could put in a big garden for all of us. There are lots of tools in the barn."

"We'd love you to live here with us, and you can do anything you want with Bertha in the forest, as long as we don't take down a healthy tree without planting three more. Remember that was always Grandma's rule," Willow said.

"No, you two own this land. Grandma put you in charge of it. Your dad and I are just here to help you do whatever you want, but we would like a safe path to this beautiful place," their mom said as they came to a clearing.

The four of them stood still, listening to the birds singing in the trees, the waterfall as it splashed into the lake, the three cats meowing as they chased frogs on the grassy banks. The lake was over an acre wide, with the mountain rising sharply along two sides and a natural bank of moss and ferns encircling the rest. Dense forest came within ten feet of the Lake.

"It's beautiful," Willow exclaimed as she slipped her shoes off her feet. "Can I dive in?"

"Not here. It's deeper in some parts than others. I'll show you the best place to dive," Laurel said as she pulled her dress over her head and stood in her bathing suit. Laurel walked to the edge closest to the waterfall and then gently dove into the lake. The three of them followed her without hesitation.

Willow came to the surface calling out to the others, "It's colder than I thought it would be."

"The lake doesn't get much sun to warm up, but it's refreshing, especially if you've been walking on the Appalachian Trail. Can you imagine? Your dad and I climbed north of here up to the campsite Grandma sent you to. It's a quarter mile up that trail, and the view was spectacular. The highway is three miles west of this lake. You could build Nuhema's Landing anywhere around here. Now you see why we want goats and sheep. They'll eat all the vines and clear out the ground so we can help you make a campsite here. Your dad can use Bertha to level the ground. We could plant grass or bring in sand for a beach. You could have a beautiful campground if you wanted."

"It shouldn't cost a lot of money. We'll pay for it when we sell the house, and you can pay us back when you get Grandma's inheritance," their dad offered.

"That money is yours," Tracy said. "You should use it to make you happy."

"We both have good retirement checks and social security coming in every month," Brian explained. "We've always been minimalists. We don't want more stuff to worry about, but a bigger lake? Now that's something worth having," he said, floating on his back, "one big enough for a kayak."

"A bigger lake and a kayak?" Willow asked, swimming over to her mom. "How much bigger? Do you both want a kayak?"

"He wants a kayak to fish from, I want a stationary float so I can swim out and sunbathe," Laurel admitted. "Your dad's been looking it up on Pinterest and thinks he can build it with a ladder for us to climb up."

"I love that idea," Tracy agreed.

"A bigger lake, the float or the kayak?" Brian asked.

"All of them," Willow said. "Does the lake have fish in it now? How could it?"

"It does. I looked it up, and fish eggs can come in with the water or on the feet of birds. A flock of Canadian Geese landed here two days ago. They stayed for a day and then took off migrating north, we think. I'd like to stock the lake with some bass and trout. Not too many, but wouldn't that be great?" Brian asked.

"I love to fish," Tracy added. "So do you, Willow. When Dad taught us how to cast from the banks, you caught that big bass that Dad had mounted."

They all started laughing as they treaded water in the center of the lake. "The mice systematically ate anything that was fish off the mounting, and all we had left was the piece of lead they had put inside the fish on a board," Willow recalled.

"That's when we got Orange Cat," Laurel added. "Thank goodness for the mice. Where are those cats?"

They all scanned the bank, finally seeing Orange Cat and the kittens eating something on the bank. "Look, they caught little minnows or tadpoles."

"Wouldn't it be wonderful to swim to my big float and sit down to talk and relax?" Laurel asked.

"Yes, it would. Let's swim to shore," Brian suggested. "We can sit on the rocks over there."

Nineteen

They climbed up a few rocks and sat down, looking out onto the lake. "Where would we put the campground?" Willow asked.

"I think on the west side of the lake. The campers would have privacy from the highway. It would be nice to provide showers and washing machines for them sometime in the future. It wouldn't have to be a big building, more like the area they have for truck drivers to use on the highway. Go to a truck stop while you're driving to the festivals. You'll get ideas," their dad suggested.

"Let's talk about the float Mom wants. I think we might as well have a big one built now."

"Can someone bring it in on a truck?" Tracy asked.

"No, I want to build it," Brian insisted. "I'll need help, but your Mom and I had a good idea."

"We've been mentioning sheep because when Morgan, Phoenix, and Jay were here, you were gushing over the baby, so I took Jay to see our trailer. He loved it. Did you know that Morgan and Jay are having a tiny home built for them?" Brian asked. "It's almost done, and it's on wheels."

"Jay told us they wanted to live in the woods when he was doing our tattoo. That was before he knew about our forest," Tracy remembered.

"I asked him where they're going to put it," Brian went on to say. "They're going to rent a place in a trailer camp until they can save enough for land."

"You dad said they want to find land in the woods where they can have three sheep," Laurel said. "It seems Morgan not only paints, but she also spins and dyes yarn to make wall hangings. She knows all about sheep and preparing the wool. She had sheep when she was in 4-H," Laurel added. "Jay could help your dad build the float."

"I'd love Morgan and Jay to live here, but I don't want to sell any land and break up our forest. What about you, Tracy?" Willow asked.

"Once we start that, the whole forest will become a housing development," Tracy agreed.

"No one should buy land, but you could let them live on it if they agree to help us take care and protect the forest. It's too much for the four of us," Laurel added. "In the barn, Grandma posted a big sign that gave us this idea. It shows what a forest village looks like, with everyone busy doing something to help support and maintain the community."

"Maybe we could find a nice person with a food truck who would want to live here when the trail is open and go south when it is closed?" Willow suggested.

"We meet food vendors at the festivals. One just had a baby, and I bet they'd love to live here. I really liked them," Tracy added.

"You loved the baby," Willow said, shaking her head and smiling. "They were a nice couple, but we wouldn't have to decide on who until the campsite is open. We'll have a few summers to spend around the vendors to find the perfect family and food truck."

"Let's ask Jay, Morgan, and Phoenix to dinner tomorrow night. We can talk it over with them. We've known Jay all our life, and I trust them both," Willow suggested.

"Does this mean Phoenix would be living here?" Tracy said, clasping her hands against her heart. "I can't believe how wonderful that would be. Our family would have a baby."

"We're scheduled to leave in four days for the Find The Cure Concert in Culpeper, Virginia. Then we were going to take a two-day vacation in Pigeon Forge, Tennessee, to go to Dollywood," Willow explained.

"We don't have to go," Tracy said. "We have so much going on."

"No. You have to go and enjoy your life," Laurel insisted. "Don't change your plans. We will all talk to Jay and Morgan tomorrow and figure out if it works."

"Can I stock a few fish in the pond?" Brian said before leaving the rocks.

"Of course," Tracy said, "and buy a kayak for Lake Wilson. What do you think of that name, Willow?"

"It's perfect. Why don't you buy Mom a rubber raft to use until you make her a permanent one?" Willow suggested. "We're so happy you are going to live here."

Late Thursday afternoon, Willow and Tracy pulled into the festival gates in Culpeper, Virginia.

"You must be the Hot-Hooping Sisters," a young man stated, as he took out his list.

"Yes, I guess we are," Willow replied.

He looked into Willow's eyes, neither saying a word. Tracy could sense the intensity of their exchange, so she smiled and looked out the opposite window. A horn blew behind them, and the man signaled the car to wait. "You're now listed as performers, so there's no charge for camping. We saw all the YouTubes from The Quarry Festival. He handed them a slip of paper with the number of their vendor spot and campsite. "We hope you'll be willing to perform on stage with a few of the bands. Our stage is made of concrete, and it's wide enough to accommodate your fire-hoops."

"Yes, certainly," Willow said, blushing as she took the paper from his hand. "Thanks for the opportunity. Do I pay our vendor fee here?"

"No, I'll stop by your site and pick it up later," he promised. "The line is getting long."

"Hot-Hooping Sisters? Who came up with that name?" Tracy said, laughing while looking at her iPhone. "Here, they are! One guy must have named us, and everyone is using it to post their videos. We do look hot!" Tracy admitted. "Pull over and look at this one. Remember when the band kept speeding up the beat to throw us off but we kept up? We were hooping so fast that it looks like a ring of fire, not five wicks burning. We look like Hot-Hooping Sisters!"

"We do," Willow admitted. "Let's keep the name."

"I don't think we have a choice," Tracy agreed. "Speaking of hotness, what about that man back there? He couldn't take his eyes off you."

"I know," Willow admitted. "I felt mesmerized."

"He's stopping by to pick up our vendor fee," Tracy reminded her. "I bet it's later tonight when the gate closes and the musicians have their mic check on stage."

"The last thing I need is a man right now," Willow stated. "You give him the check when he stops by."

"The only thing you need is a man," Tracy said. "Enjoy yourself. Flirt a little. You deserve it."

They set up their tent and moved the van to their vendor space. Their site was next to the food vendor who sold fish sandwiches. "The cats are going to love this," Willow said.

"Everybody is getting something. What's my fun surprise?" Tracy teased, and then she saw the family with the baby were vendors on the other side. "I'll be right back."

Willow was disappointed when the man never came by their booth or tent site. The gates had been closed and the first band to perform tomorrow was set up on stage getting ready for their mic check. A crowd had gathered and was urging them to play a few songs. Willow and Tracy grabbed their lite-up hoops and went to see the show.

The band tuned up their instruments and then the leader used the mic to call out, "Tucker. Are you ready for us?"

The man from the gate came on stage, moved a few mics around and asked the crowd, "Are we ready for them?"

Everyone yelled, "Yes, play something."

Willow dropped her hoop, so Tracy picked it up, flipped the switch on, and handed it back to her. "Come on, Sis. We're going on stage with Tucker."

As the band started playing, both sisters took the stage, one on each side of the group. The crowd clapped and hooted appreciation. Five songs later, the mini-concert was over, and the crowd dispersed to get rest before the long days ahead. Tracy walked back with two friends she'd met at The Quarry. Willow walked with Tucker.

"So you're the man in charge?" Willow asked.

"No, I'm just in charge of the sound and stage, but I help out wherever needed," he admitted. "It's my summer job. I'm just a poor college kid."

"My sister and I are going to start night school for massage this fall. We'll work at a hospital taking blood until we get through."

"How long will it take you?" Tucker asked.

"Two years," Willow explained. "How about you?"

"I'm a senior. I'll be done next year," he answered. "What do you know, we have a lot in common."

Another band saw Tucker and called out to him. "Hey, Tucker! You got a minute?" Willow walked on alone with a smile on her face and a flutter in her heart.

The two concert days were hot and sticky, but crowds of people braved the heat. Women bought tie-dyed shirts to keep the sun off their shoulders, and sixty hula hoops found new homes. The stand also attracted kids who painted rocks and bought the feather hair clips. The sisters hula-hooped to the music at their booth and became the Hot-Hooping Sisters at night.

In the afternoon of the last day, rain and cold weather blew in. The crowd hurried to their cars and pulled out of the gates. Tucker's festival outfit had been jeans, a bare-chest, and a headband and feather. He was tan and muscular and now stood shivering in front of Willow's table.

"Come in under our canopy," Willow suggested. "I still owe you our vendor fee. Here's the check," she said.

"Thanks. You did a lot to make this a success. I should give the fee back to you," Tucker suggested.

"The people that run this might not like that," Willow said. "Keep it, we all worked hard." They looked at each other, at a loss for words until Willow insisted. "Tucker, take this shirt. You're freezing." She handed him a tie-dyed shirt and added, "Here's our card. My phone number's on it."

Tucker smiled, put the shirt on, then reached out and drew her to him in a warm hug. "I'll call you," he whispered in her ear.

The next day, the sisters checked into their hotel room in Pigeon Forge, Tennessee, changed into their swimsuits and were leaving for the pool when Willow's phone rang. She picked it up and told Tracy, "I think it's Tucker. What do I do?"

"I don't know about you," Tracy said laughing, "but I'm on vacation. I'm going to go swimming while you answer that phone, Sis."

Half an hour later, Willow jumped in the pool next to Tracy, who had been lying peacefully on a pool raft. "You splashed me," Tracy complained. "I think pools are boring. We can't take our cats out. There's no fish around my feet, no frogs singing on the sides, no turtles sunbathing. I'm surrounded by blue concrete. It's no Wilson Lake. What did Tucker want?"

"He's in charge of the sound and lights at a two-day psychedelic concert in Ohio. He says we'd sell lots of tie-dye shirts and hula hoops. It starts Saturday so we'd have to stay here an extra day and then drive to Ohio Friday. Do we have enough stock left?"

"I filled Mom's van with most of our merchandise. While you were driving, I checked what's left. We have around two hundred tee shirts, seventy-five hula hoops, lots of rocks and a big box of hair ties. If we sell it all, we'll be out of stock. We better order more supplies while we're on the road and start making stuff as soon as we get home."

"So you think we should go?" Willow asked.

"Of course," Tracy said. "I get to spend another day in Pigeon Forge. That means we can buy a two-day ticket to Dollywood and do the theme park and Splash Country. We'll have one day left to tour her hometown and the Smoky Mountains. Then we'll go to Ohio to sell lots of merchandise while you get more time with Tucker. I like the two of you together."

"Why?" Willow asked, amazed.

"You're so much alike," Tracy continued. "You're both shy, don't talk too much and are hard workers. Plus you're both crazy over each other."

"No way," Willow insisted. "I hardly know the man."

"All the more reason for us to go to Ohio on Friday," Tracy said.

They were among the first to arrive at Dollywood Park, so they didn't have to wait in line to get in. Tracy had mapped out their entire day and led the way through a beautiful village to one building. "What's in here?" Willow asked.

"It's rated with five stars. I think it's a wooden roller coaster," Tracy answered. "How bad can it be if it's wood?"

"We've never been on a mechanical ride," Willow reminded her as they moved through a series of walkways toward a loud sound. "Grandma wouldn't let us go on carnival rides because she didn't think they were safe."

"I trust Dolly Parton with my life. Let's live a little, Sis," Tracy said, and she dragged her onto the world's fastest wooden roller coaster. They screamed as it rocketed them around massive turns, twists, and drops. They were airborne for nearly twenty seconds. When it stopped, they could hardly catch their breath but managed to scramble out with the help of two other women.

"I'm shaking," Willow said as she grabbed one of the women's hands. "Help my sister, please." Another woman helped Tracy, and the four of them left laughing and talking about the adventure.

"Did you like it?" one asked.

"I'm not sure," Tracy admitted. "I've never experienced anything like it. What a shock."

"Come with us. You need to ride The Wild Eagle. It's our favorite. Do you mind heights?" one woman asked.

"No, we live in the mountains, why?" Willow inquired as they ran.

"You'll feel like you're flying. It goes sixty-one miles per hour, and there's a two hundred and ten-foot drop. It's fantastic."

They spent the day riding all the thrill rides. Late in the day, they said goodbye to the two women who had acted as their guides and went to a restaurant to eat. "I can't handle one more ride," Willow said after ordering.

"I can't either, but what an amazing experience," Tracy admitted. "After we eat I want to go to Dolly's Museum. It's what I'm most looking forward to. It's not far from here, and it's air-conditioned."

As they strolled from one gorgeous room into another, Tracy stared at Dolly's elaborate costumes without speaking. She read every placard and teared up several times. When they approached the glass case with the original Coat of Many Colors, Tracy's tears rolled down her cheeks. "Look," she whispered. "Her mom made her that coat out of little pieces of rags. I would have dressed that way if it wasn't for you."

"Dolly didn't care," Willow pointed out. "She felt rich because she had love. You were loved by your mom and all of us. You were never poor."

The last day they started out exploring the Smoky Mountain Arts and Crafts Loop. The sisters stopped to admire the work of woodworkers, jewelers, potters, spinners, and artists. They bought sandwiches and drinks and drove into the National Smoky Mountain Park. They toured for an hour, looking out the car windows at a black bear and her cubs, horse riders, and beautiful natural scenery. They pulled over and sat by a stream, took out their lunch, and listened to the sounds of the birds and water.

"This has been an adventure of a lifetime," Tracy said. "Thank you. I see the world so differently now, but I feel happiest here in the forest. I miss home."

"You do?" Willow asked, amazed. "I'm sitting here thinking about where we can go next. I love exploring new places. I could live on the road for the rest of my life."

"Not me," Tracy replied. "I'll enjoy the festivals and traveling this summer, but I want a little home in the woods like Morgan and Jay are getting. I might take a pottery class so I can make bowls as Grandma did. Maybe her wheel is still in the barn. Did you see how that woman made it go with her feet?"

Just then, Willow's phone rang, and she smiled. "It's Tucker," she announced as she got up and moved away for privacy. When she returned, her face was glowing. "I asked him to tell me a little about himself. He said his webpage tells everything I would ever want to know and more. He sent me the link. Seems he creates webpages for people in addition to his work at shows. I'm afraid to look," Willow admitted.

The sisters sat side by side as she took out her phone and opened his webpage. The first line read, *My dream is to see the world.* Tracy smiled and said, "Looks like you found someone as curious as you."

Epilogue

Five years later, a hiker hobbled into the Nuhema Massage Studio. A tall, good-looking man greeted him with, "Welcome. My name is Keith. How long have you been on the trail?"

"Three months. I can't believe this place. I feel like I found heaven on earth."

"We hear that from a lot of hikers. When did you arrive?" Keith asked.

"I was determined to get here, but I arrived at dusk. When I woke up, I couldn't believe that the rumors about this place are true. My name's Roger," he added.

"Looks like you cleaned up," Keith suggested.

"Once I set up my tent, I washed my clothes and showered twice. I just came from a long swim in the lake. I've been told you can help me with my feet and torn muscles. Can I make an appointment?" Roger asked.

"No problem. I've got an opening at four today. In the meantime, you can grab something to eat from the food truck, pick up supplies at the hiker store, and shop at the Arts and Craft Gallery. They ship anything you buy to your home. I suggest that you come back at three. You need to soak your feet for an hour in our footbath. We use a solution designed for hikers by the top podiatrist at Harrisburg Hospital. Then at four, I can make those aches and pains go away."

"Sounds good," Roger said as he stared at one picture on the wall. "Does the artist that painted this sell her work in the gallery?"

"Yes, Morgan does. Her work sells out quickly," Keith stated.

"Who is the woman in this painting? I love her face, and the way she seems to want to get to know me. I feel welcomed," Roger said.

"That's Nuhema, the woman who owned all this land and foresaw Nuhema's landing."

"What does Nuhema mean?" Roger asked without taking his eyes off the painting.

"She was a Lenape Indian and Nuhema means Grandma in her language. She left the land to her two granddaughters," Keith explained as he pointed to a few pictures.

"These are the Hot-Hooping Sisters. I saw them at a concert years ago. They were amazing. Do they work here?" he asked hopefully.

"They own this studio and all of Nuhema's Landing. They built it from the ground up. Neither of them is here today. This one is my wife, Tracy. She's home resting because we're expecting in a few weeks. It's twins so they may come early."

"You're a lucky man. Do you know what you're having?" Roger asked.

"Yes, twin girls. I am blessed," he said, looking at the pictures with the young man.

"I think her name is Willow," Roger said as he pointed his finger. "Is she here?"

"It gets lonely on the trail, doesn't it?" Keith teased.

Keith walked over to another wall and looked at an itinerary. "According to this schedule, Willow and her boyfriend, Tucker, are in Cuba riding horses through a tobacco field up to a cigar factory. They're bringing back cigars to celebrate when the girls are born."

I hope you enjoyed this book. If you did, please Facebook me, Pamela H. Bender. I'd like to hear from you. Meanwhile, I am home, writing the next book in The Ripple Effect series entitled Nuhema's Landing.

About the Author

Pamela H. Bender spent most of her career in education crafting words to help children. She wrote grants, testified in congressional hearings and worked on legislation for the students of an inner-city school district. Her first two series were written for adults. Writing a new series for teens and adults is a natural progression in her writing career.

Following her own advice, she lives each day to the fullest. By the time her husband, Joe, wakes up, she's immersed in the flow of creation. If she's taking a long walk with their Mini Australian Shepherd, Josey, he knows she's working on a plot twist. If their orange cat, Millie, is on the back of her chair, he knows Pam is writing.

Her children have always been the center of her private life. Twenty-three grandchildren and seven married kids keep her busy and connected to the complex world of teens. Some of the problems they face show up on the pages of this novel, and some come from her own experiences. The light-hearted adventures come from Heidi Glunt.

Pam hopes the books in The Ripple Effect series will both empower teens and increase communication between the generations.

She would love to hear from you. Feel free to message her on Facebook, Pamela H. Bender, or email her at pam45@comcast.net.

Other Titles by the Author

LIVING PASSIONATELY

BOOK ONE: Jo is an orphan and although only five feet tall, she owns, breeds, grooms, trains, and races horses on the farm she inherited. She's bound and determined to save her reputation and achieve her father's last dream by going for the win. When a southern vet strides into her barn, Jo is reminded that life has more to offer than just winning races.

BOOK TWO: Bess, a young widow, is determined to focus only on six-year-old Sadie. Relocating to Pennsylvania, Bess teaches spinning at a yarn shop. Just when they are settling into their new life, fate and three circling vultures instantly change everything.

BOOK THREE: When Aurora comes home from the Army to take over her father's stained-glass studio, she becomes the linchpin for change in her city. Trained to defend, she reacts automatically to take on two armed men, and just may get sucked into the seedy underbelly of crime.

THE DENNISON FAMILY SAGA

PREQUEL: When Protestant Varena marries a Catholic, it's anyone's guess how her tight-knit German family will react. Will the birth of their child, Ron Dennison, bring about peace and unity, or will religion divide them further? Join Ron and his father, Harold, in their petticoat-governed household as this beautiful family tale unfolds.

BOOK ONE: Mimi Dennison loses her mother the day she is born. Her father unable to care for her or her two-year-old sister, she becomes a vagabond ward of the extended family. Separated from her sister and passed from family to family, Mimi develops her own unique blend of survival skills, personality quirks, and thirst for adventure in this Roaring Twenties coming-of-age novel.

BOOK TWO: Ron and Mimi Dennison welcome the arrival of their second daughter, Anna, along with a stream of returning GIs moving to their fledgling Long Island neighborhood at the close of World War II. Rising Up gives voice to a powerful anthem that rails against violence and victimization as it embraces the process of freeing oneself from abuse.

BOOK THREE: Anna has sworn off dating until she runs into an old friend, Jeb Derben. A newly widowed retired elementary principal, he shares Anna's friends, contacts and core values. Jeb likes the simple life with no frills. He's a straight talker who learned life lessons while growing up in a house attached to the family bar and dance hall. Taking one last leap of faith, Anna marries Jeb and starts a new chapter in her life.

www.ingramcontent.com/pod-product-compliance
Lightning Source LLC
Chambersburg PA
CBHW020636180626
46816CB00003B/998